"I can't ask you ... care of two very lively—"

"You're not asking. I'm offering. It's important that you finish school."

"Be that as it may, you will have enough on your hands taking care of your grandmother. I don't want anyone's pity." Amber's cheeks pinked. "You have no idea how humiliating it is to always be on the receiving end of charity."

Something tore in Ethan's heart. Then inspiration struck. He leaned forward. "What if we were to make a mutually beneficial deal?"

She gave him a look. "You and your deals."

"What if we could do each other a favor?"

Her forehead creased. "I don't understand."

"Grandma is going to need more care than I can provide. What if you helped her? In turn, I could watch the girls so you can finish school."

"You're proposing an exchange of services?"

"Exactly. No charity involved."

She studied him for a long moment. "I guess there's no harm in giving it a try."

Lisa Carter and her family make their home in North Carolina. In addition to her Love Inspired novels, she writes romantic suspense for Abingdon Press. When she isn't writing, Lisa enjoys traveling to romantic locales, teaching writing workshops and researching her next exotic adventure. She has strong opinions on barbecue and ACC basketball. She loves to hear from readers. Connect with Lisa at lisacarterauthor.com.

Books by Lisa Carter

Love Inspired

Visit the Author Profile page at Harlequin.com.

The Twin Bargain

Lisa Carter

HARLEQUIN® LOVE INSPIRED®

Recycling programs
for this product may
not exist in your area.

 LOVE INSPIRED BOOKS

ISBN-13: 978-1-335-47948-8

The Twin Bargain

www.Harlequin.com

Printed in U.S.A.

And we know that all things work together for good to them that love God, to them who are the called according to his purpose.
—*Romans* 8:28

Chapter One

Ethan Green had feared this day coming, almost as long as he could remember.

The double glass doors whooshed shut behind him. An antiseptic smell assaulted his nostrils. On the intercom, someone paged a doctor. An orderly pushed a squeaky cart past Ethan.

Heart pounding, he headed straight for the information desk. "Can you give me the room number for Erma-Jean Hicks, please?"

"I'll be with you in a minute." The volunteer answered the ringing phone. "Truelove Medical Center..." Ignoring him, the woman scrolled through the computer monitor.

He bit back his frustration. Beads of sweat peppered his forehead. A dozen scenarios, each one worse than the last, flashed through his brain. What had happened to Grandma Hicks?

A broken hip? A stroke? A heart attack?

Suppose she'd passed? Suppose he'd missed saying goodbye? Suppose he never got to tell her how much he—

"Ethan? Is that you?"

Amber Fleming's blue eyes—the same blue as her hospital scrubs—widened and locked on to his. Something entirely painful zinged inside his chest.

Her hair the color of winter wheat, she remained as tall—or in her case as small—as he remembered. But other than her ponytail, the pesky tagalong he recalled from high school was long gone. A pink stethoscope draped around her neck, she looked very professional.

Ethan flushed. "You're a nurse?"

She touched the photo ID badge clipped to her tunic. "Nursing student." She tilted her head, setting the ponytail aquiver. "Matt didn't tell you?"

Ethan tore his gaze from the silky blond hair brushing her shoulder. "No, he didn't."

He and Amber's older brother had been best friends since they were kids. Ethan wondered what else Matt had failed to mention. His eyes cut to the bare finger of her left hand. No ring.

What was with him? This was Matt's little sister. This was Amber.

He cleared his throat. "GeorgeAnne Allen left me a message this morning to drop everything and come to Truelove. She didn't say what happened, only that my grandmother had been admitted to the hospital."

"It must've taken you all day to get to the mountains from the coast." Amber's eyes darted to the volunteer, still on the phone. "I was headed to see Miss ErmaJean. Let me take you there."

He swallowed. "Tell me the truth, Amber. Is Grandma dying?"

Amber laid her hand on his leather jacket. "She's going to be fine, Ethan." She led him through a pair of automatic doors. "Miss ErmaJean took a tumble at her house and broke her leg."

Ethan followed Amber down the white-tiled corridor. "But she's going to be okay?"

"Her leg has already been cast." Amber pushed the elevator button. "But when she fell, she also hit her head. The doctor wants to keep her at the hospital for a few days as a precaution."

The elevator doors opened, and they stepped inside.

"I want to talk to her doctor."

Amber glanced at her watch. "Unfortunately, he's probably left for the day, but if you talk to the duty nurse, she can put you in touch with him. Same info I've already given you, though."

He frowned. "Why were you informed about my grandmother's condition and not me?"

Pressing the third-floor button, she pursed her lips. "He told me because I was here."

He stiffened at her implied rebuke.

The elevator doors closed.

"I got here as soon as I could."

Ascending, the elevator lurched.

She crossed her arms. "When was the last time you visited Truelove? It's been ten years, right?"

He didn't remember Amber being this bossy or pushy. "I was deployed."

"But you've been out of the Marines for four months, Ethan."

"Not visiting Truelove isn't the same as not seeing Grandma. She's visited me in Wilmington several times." He jutted his jaw. "Not that it's any of your business."

"Where were you when Miss ErmaJean got the flu? When her identity was stolen? When—"

"I get it, Amber," he growled. "Since I returned to North Carolina, I could've been around more, but I've been looking for work."

Elevator dinging, the doors opened onto the third floor.

She stepped out. "But not looking where you have family and friends?"

He followed on her heels. "You know how I feel about this one-stoplight town. Grandma Hicks understands. Why didn't she call me when the other stuff happened?"

"Because your grandmother doesn't want to infringe on your life." Amber glared. "She doesn't want to relinquish her independence or be a burden."

He scowled back. "Grandma Hicks isn't a burden. She knows I'd do anything to help her."

"Here's your chance to prove it. Until she's mobile again, she is in no shape to live alone."

He wasn't used to Amber being ticked with him. When they were younger, she'd sort of had a crush on him. He never acted on it because she was Matt's little sister. Kind of an unspoken guy rule. That and he enjoyed breathing. Amber's dad was overprotective.

"The doctor says she'll need physical therapy. The cast probably won't come off for six weeks." Amber's eyes narrowed. "No doubt, you'll be long gone by then. But Miss ErmaJean has lots of friends who will look out for her."

Amber's low opinion of him stung.

"I'll take care of my grandmother." He squared his shoulders. "This incident settles it. I'm moving her to Wilmington."

Amber's eyes widened. "You can't do that, Ethan."

He drew himself up. "I *can* do that, Amber. And I'll make sure she gets the best of care."

Amber shook her head. "She'll hate it. She'll miss Miss GeorgeAnne and Miss IdaLee. Her house. Her church. The mountains."

"You and those old women should mind your own business." He cocked his head. "I'll take care of Grandma."

Hurt flashed through those sky-blue eyes of hers. Her lips trembled. And he felt about two inches tall.

She was only looking out for his grandmother. But she'd hit a nerve. He wasn't his deadbeat dad. He'd never be him. Grandma Hicks had practically raised him by herself.

Amber stopped outside the second door on the right. "Here's her room."

He'd been harsh. Anger had always been his fallback, rather than fear.

"I'm sorry." He scrubbed his face with his hand. "I didn't mean to bark at you. Thanks for showing me the way to Grandma's room."

There were purple shadows under Amber's eyes. She looked tired. And, at twenty-six, older than she should. Nursing school must be exhausting.

She bit her lip. "I was headed here, anyway."

Ethan steeled himself for what he'd discover on the other side. But what he found wasn't anything like what he expected.

His heart in his throat, he pushed through the door to find his rosy-cheeked grandmother lying propped against the pillows. And two little ash-blonde girls—twins?— standing on either side of the bed.

The sight of his pleasantly plump grandmother in the hospital bed caused his heart to swell with unexpected gladness. Apple round, his grandma was what he liked to think of as fluffy. Her salt-and-pepper hair was no whiter than when she'd visited him over the winter.

"Ethan?" Catching sight of him, Grandma Hicks's face lifted. "Oh, honey, it's so good to see you."

Behind him, Amber slipped inside the room. "Lucy. Stella." She held out her hand.

The little girl in lavender let go of the bedrail and ducked behind Amber. The one in pink maintained her hold on the steel bar and peered at Ethan.

"Grandma, are you all right?" He took her blue-veined hand. Her skin felt warm to the touch.

She squeezed his fingers. "GeorgeAnne shouldn't have bothered you. I'm fine."

"You are not fine." An uncustomary emotion clogged his throat. "And you're not a bother."

"I'll be right as rain, give or take a few weeks." She patted his arm. "Can't keep a good woman down for long."

The little girl in pink came around the end of the bed, bypassing Amber. "Gigi got hurt."

Ethan raised his eyebrows. "Gigi?"

His grandmother's cheeks dimpled. "Closest I could get to Great-Gran."

Ethan frowned. "Who do these children belong to, Grandma?"

"Me."

His gaze flicked to Amber and then to the child beside him. His mouth opened and closed. The adorable little girl gave him a bright smile, and his breath caught. She was the spitting image of Amber at that age.

Sky-blue eyes. From the tip of her tiny nose and stalwart little chin, same as her mother. A mini-Amber.

Grandma Hicks reached through the railing and touched the child's hand. "Lucy, this is my grandson, Ethan. The one I told you about."

Out of the corner of her lashes, Lucy looked at him. "Hey, mister."

Sunshine. Warmth. And a sense of well-being flooded over him.

"It—it's Ethan." He cleared his throat, glancing from his grandmother to this slender princess of a child. "Telling tales about me, Grandma?"

"Only the truth."

He rolled his eyes. "That's what I was afraid of."

"The good things. The stuff you don't like to think people know."

He tried to wrap his mind around a grown-up Amber with children of her own. "Matt never told me you have daughters."

"Like on the ark, they came in twos. This is Stella." Amber stepped aside, giving him a clearer look at the child hunkered next to her mother. "Stella, this is Ethan, Uncle Matt's best friend."

Pert nose. Dimpled chin. Identical to her sister. Yet somehow not. A person entirely in her own right.

The notion of Amber being married left him with an unsettled feeling in his gut.

"You just missed Callie, Amber." Grandma smiled. "I didn't want her to miss the golden photography hour for her client's engagement pictures so I sent her off. I knew you'd be here soon."

"I was so relieved Callie was available to pick up the girls from school this afternoon. She texted me she'd dropped the girls off here. I came over as soon as I finished my shift at the diner. She said the twins were worried." Amber sighed. "I know they feel so bad about what happened this morning."

Ethan frowned. "The girls were there when Grandma fell?"

Grandma rested her palm on Lucy's silken head.

"Lucy and Stella were wonderful. They called 911, like their mommy taught them to do in an emergency."

Ethan stared at his grandmother. "You've been baby-sitting Amber's children?" His voice rose.

"We're not babies." The silent twin let go of her mother and folded her little arms across her chest. "We're four years old."

"Of course you're not babies, Stella darling. You are my two most favorite big girls." Grandma Hicks threw him a warning look. "They also managed to call their honorary aunt Callie. I'm so thankful she was able to get to my house, even before the ambulance arrived. You remember Callie, don't you, Ethan?"

"Yeah," he grunted. Callie's family owned the Apple Valley orchard. Callie and Matt had dated in high school.

"She's Maisie's mommy," Lucy said.

Callie Jackson had a kid, too? She'd been Amber's best friend since they were children. A couple of years older, Ethan and Matt had spent a great deal of their growing-up years at either the orchard or the Fleming family white-water rafting business.

"The Jacksons still own the orchard, but she's Callie McAbee now." A smile tugged the corners of his grandmother's lips. "And did the Double Name Club ever have a time getting her and Jake together. But all's well that ends well."

His thoughts on the Double Name Club—more notoriously known as the Truelove Matchmakers—were best left unvoiced. GeorgeAnne Allen. IdaLee Moore. ErmaJean Hicks.

The sixtysomething ladies were infamous for poking their powdered noses where they didn't belong. They took the town motto—Truelove, Where True Love Awaits—a little too seriously.

Apparently, gentle, auburn-haired Callie Jackson had been their latest victim. He felt a surge of empathy for the unknown Jake McAbee. Fortunately for Ethan, he'd always been too much of a black sheep for the ladies to ever target him.

Then as if on cue, the uncontested leader of the matchmaker pack, Miss GeorgeAnne, poked her nose into the hospital room. "Reporting for duty."

Amber bristled. Angular and bony, GeorgeAnne had that effect on people. "I think it best if I take the girls home myself, Miss GeorgeAnne."

Married, divorced or spinster, the "Miss" was an honorary title of respect bestowed on any Southern lady who was your elder. No matter if the "Miss" was elderly or not.

"Nonsense. You needn't miss your class." The old woman's glacier-blue eyes sparked over the twins. "I figure if nothing else, the girls and I can sort a bucket of bolts at the hardware store."

Lucy's eyes rounded.

Stella's rosebud lips flattened. "No bolts, Miss G'Anne."

Good for her. He felt a ridiculous, misplaced pride. Another Truelove rebel in the making. GeorgeAnne wasn't exactly his definition of maternal. He felt bad for the girls.

Amber's face tightened. "I should've never allowed you to talk me into this, Miss ErmaJean. The girls are my responsibility. Why did I ever think I could—"

"It's been a trying day, but I won't let you throw in the stethoscope over this little bump in the road." Grandma waved her hand. "If you hurry, you can still get to class on time."

Ethan rocked on his heels. "I don't know what's going

on here, but I'd say your leg in a cast is more than a bump in the road, Grandma."

His grandmother lifted her chin. "What's going on here is that Amber's come too far in her nursing studies to quit now."

"Miss ErmaJean—"

"It's settled." Grandma Hicks shrugged. "At least for tonight. We'll work out something. Don't you worry, sweetheart."

He grimaced. "Why can't your husband take care of the girls, Amber?"

Lucy tugged at his jacket. "We don't have a daddy, Efan."

And the bottom fell out of his stomach.

GeorgeAnne pursed her thin lips. Grandma looked like she wanted to strangle him. Without meaning to, he'd put his foot in it.

The shock at seeing Ethan again was not dissimilar to the stinging jolt Amber had felt when once she overturned one of her father's rafts into the freezing cold water of the river.

But the sensation was the same. Fighting her way to the surface, gasping for air. Her heart in overdrive. This couldn't be real. *He* couldn't be real.

Amber shook herself slightly, trying to clear her muddled thoughts. Ethan Green wasn't an illusion. Standing beside Miss ErmaJean's hospital bed, he was as real and solid as the granite rocks of the North Carolina mountains.

She tried not to gape at him. The broad shoulders, the well-muscled chest beneath the jacket, the six-pack waist that tapered to his jeans. This man she didn't know—the man who'd fulfilled the youthful potential of the boy she'd once loved so impossibly. This man robbed her of coherent thought.

Amber wasn't sure why her brother hadn't told Ethan about the last five years of her life. When he and Matt left for basic training, she believed she'd never see Ethan again. His leave-taking had been so final. He'd been so exultant about finally gaining his freedom from the small-town life he hated.

Freedom. A concept she barely remembered. She tucked a loose tendril of hair behind her ear. His gaze followed the motion of her hand. And something fluttered like the wings of a butterfly inside her rib cage.

Ethan's gold-flecked hazel eyes were as intense as ever. She swallowed against the rush of feeling. What was wrong with her?

He'd surprised her, that's all. She hadn't expected to see him here. Not after so much time. No big deal.

Especially on a day like today when her plans to make a better life for her children were falling to pieces.

She endeavored to get her traitorous heart to settle down. No easy task when it came to the boy she'd had a schoolgirl crush on since she was... Eleven?

As far back as memory served, there'd been her, Matt, Ethan and Callie. Inseparable. Or that's what she'd believed until Ethan made a deal with Matt, convincing her brother to also join the Marines after graduation.

She and Callie had been left behind. At sixteen, she'd never dreamed being left behind would become the story of her life. She finished growing up alone, the hard way. Experience, a bitter teacher.

Why was he staring at her? Self-conscious, she smoothed her hand over her scrubs. Well aware the years hadn't been kind. But he could at least pretend not to look so...so shocked.

Was it her appearance or single motherhood that shocked him the most? Her ex-husband, Lucy and Stella's father, had been an irresponsible jerk, but she worked hard to make sure the twins never suffered for her errors in judgment.

She fingered the end of the stethoscope. "Girls, tell everyone good-night."

"Night-night, Gigi." Lucy smiled at Ethan. "You, too, Efan."

Stella glued herself to Amber's leg.

"I was kidding about the bolts." GeorgeAnne planted her hands on her bony hips. "I've heard you two girls like milkshakes. I wasn't misinformed, was I? Thought we might swing by the drive-through on the way to your house."

Lucy immediately abandoned Ethan. "I wike vani-waa, Miss G'Anne."

Stella made a face. "I like strawberry-vanilla-chocolate ice cream."

GeorgeAnne's mouth quirked. "Who doesn't?"

Amber quickly calculated how much money her depleted wallet contained. Not enough for milkshakes. "I'm sorry, girls, but—"

GeorgeAnne raised her hand. "My treat. Got nothing but a passel of grandsons. I think it's time to see how the other half lives."

Amber warmed toward the often sharp-tongued, overly brusque woman. "Thank you, Miss GeorgeAnne." For not making her feel like such a charity case.

The older woman moved toward the door. "The train for milkshakes is leaving now. Anyone going to hop on board?"

"Me!" Lucy grabbed hold of her sister's hand. "Steh-waa, too."

Amber's heart sank. Stella looked like she'd rather eat

live worms. Her babies had made so many sacrifices so she could finish school and get a good job.

Doing her best to ignore Ethan and her zinging pulse, Amber ushered the odd trio to the elevator.

Until Miss ErmaJean offered to take care of Lucy and Stella, she'd struggled to juggle her waitress job, single parenting and nursing school. It was good of Miss GeorgeAnne to babysit the girls, but with ErmaJean out of commission, tonight would have to be her last class.

The twins and Miss GeorgeAnne stepped into the elevator.

Only two months left till graduation. But there was no other option. She'd have to withdraw from the program.

Lucy waved goodbye. Stella glowered. As the elevator doors closed, the rest of Amber's life stretched out before her in a bleak panorama.

Endless shifts at the Mason Jar. The broken-down trailer. Never quite making ends meet. Once again, it would be her girls who suffered the most for her mistakes.

Her shoulders slumped. She was so tired of battling life alone. "Is this all there ever will be for me and the girls, God?" she whispered.

She passed her hand over her face. It wasn't like Amber to be melancholy. She was a fighter. Scrappy, Ethan used to say. But right now, she felt the fight had been beaten out of her.

Yet she wasn't alone. She had wonderful friends like Miss ErmaJean and Callie. God had never left her. He wouldn't fail her now, even with this seemingly insurmountable setback.

After all this time, seeing Ethan revived memories and dreams she'd believed long buried. Emotions she had no time, energy or right to feel. And Ethan wanted to take ErmaJean away for good?

It felt like the final straw. His grandmother had become a mentor, confidante and friend. If only there was a way to convince him to let Miss ErmaJean convalesce at home.

Who was she kidding? Amber couldn't get her own life on track. Why did she think she had the right to tell anyone else how to live theirs?

Chapter Two

With the departure of GeorgeAnne, Amber and her daughters, Ethan turned again toward his grandmother. "You were watching the girls when you fell, Grandma?"

"It wasn't their fault." At the hint of censure in his voice, his grandmother pressed her lips together. "And nothing makes me happier than seeing their bright little faces."

Of late, when he'd called she'd seemed distracted—not all there. Half the time, she forgot to return his calls. And after a friend's mother was diagnosed with dementia, he'd begun to fear his beloved grandmother was slipping.

Ethan hugged her now. Reassured by the usual lavender scent that always clung to her. Somehow he'd feared she'd be frailer. Or her mind not as sharp.

But Grandma wasn't any frailer than he remembered. Her mind… Well… ErmaJean Hicks would never be accused of thinking like everybody else.

"How did you fall? Were you dizzy? Did you lose your balance?"

She fluttered her hand. "I was in a hurry. Tripped over my own clumsy feet on the back steps."

"It makes me sick to think about something happening and me not being here, Grandma."

She scanned his face. "A situation easily remedied."

"I've been doing a lot of thinking about the future lately."

She clasped her hands to her heart. "Oh, Ethan, I've been hoping, praying, you would."

He pulled a chair close to the bed. "Remember how much fun we had the last time you visited me in Wilmington?"

Confusion darkened her eyes. "Ice cream. Sand between my toes. Life is a beach."

"You know I like working with my hands."

"Granddad always hoped one day you'd take over—"

"A buddy of mine is starting his own boat repair business and has offered me a job."

Her hands fell to her lap. "I'm guessing boat repair means the job is on the coast."

"You said it yourself, Grandma—life is a beach."

"I misspoke. *Vacation* is a beach." Her expression clouded. "*Life* is home. I was hoping when you finally decided to settle down—"

"Truelove was never an option for me, and you know it."

She gnashed her teeth. "What I know is you're stubborn, obstinate and aggravating."

"Home is family. And you're the only family I've ever had."

She lifted her chin. "GeorgeAnne, IdaLee and I have some ideas on how you could remedy that situation."

The sheer thought of the matchmakers plotting to pair him to some Truelove girl was almost enough to send Ethan running for his Harley motorcycle. Or break out in hives.

Instead—as a Marine he'd been taught not to flee in the face of peril—he found his grandmother's hand through the bedrail. "Now that I'm stateside for good, I want us to spend more time together."

Her lips pursed. "That will be difficult with you six hours away."

Ethan set his jaw. "Which is why I'd like for you to relocate to the beach."

She pulled her hand from his. "Out of the question."

"Hear me out, Grandma. I've done my research. There is a great senior adult village near my apartment. You'd love the cottages. A sweet deal, right on the water. You'd have your own little garden for your flowers. I've got photos on my—"

"Absolutely not." She steepled her hands in her lap. "My life is here, Ethan. My friends. My church. The family business. They're all here."

What family business? Although his grandmother had continued to work on upholstery projects here and there, his grandfather's furniture restoration workshop had gathered dust since his death.

Ethan shook his head. "You've worked hard your entire life. With this new job, I can take care of you. You can retire and enjoy life for a change."

She crossed her arms. "I'm enjoying life right where I'm planted."

"You're the friendliest person I've ever known. You'll make lots of friends. There are amazing churches at the beach."

She narrowed her eyes. "And you would know that how, Ethan?"

Okay, she had him there. He hadn't sat in a church pew since he left Truelove.

Grandma's chin wobbled. "Besides, I could never leave your grandfather."

Ethan took a long, measured breath. "Granddad has been dead a long time. I don't like to think of you living here alone with me so far away." He gestured at the bed. "Changes need to be made."

Grandma stiffened. "I have good friends to watch out for me."

"The house has to be getting too much for you. And you must get lonely."

"Are you sure it's not *you* who's lonely?"

This wasn't going like he'd envisioned. Since leaving the Corps, he had been lonely. Actually, the empty feeling inside his chest had begun before he left the service.

"I do miss you, Grandma. Which is why you moving closer is a wonderful idea."

Her mouth down-turned. "Maybe for you. I'm not the decrepit old woman you think I am, Ethan Todd Green."

She only used his full name when he'd gotten on her last nerve.

Her eyes glinted. "If I need or want your help, I'll ask for it."

"Grandma, I'm concerned about you."

Her lips thinned. "If this accident was your only reason for finally visiting me, then you've wasted a trip home."

Ethan opened his hands. "I wanted to see you. I thought you'd be excited by my news. And I was worried about you."

Her face creased. "Why were you worried?"

"You've sounded so..." He swallowed. "So distant on the phone. Not like yourself."

Like he was losing her. His grandmother, the only anchor he'd ever known. Hence, his determination to put his plan into action.

"Other than this bum leg, I'm great." His grandmother tilted her head. "I told you I've been busy, Ethan. I've been watching Amber's kids so she can finish her nursing degree."

"Why did no one tell me that Amber is married?"

His grandmother gave him a cockeyed glance. "Didn't realize you were interested in Amber's marital status." She moistened her lips. "And it's *married* as in the past tense. When she got pregnant with the girls—"

"What happened, Grandma? To Amber and..." He made a face. "The guy."

"You mean her husband?" For a second, something appeared to amuse his grandmother. Then her smile faded. "Tony told Amber he didn't sign up for parenthood."

Just like his own deadbeat excuse for a father. Anger roiled in Ethan's belly.

"I still don't get how this involves you." He frowned. "And I'm surprised Amber asked you to take care of her children."

"Which part comes as a surprise to you?" Grandma arched her brow. "That I adore children or that I'm still capable of taking care of them?"

Somewhere he and Grandma had gotten off on the wrong foot. She appeared determined to take offense at every turn.

"Amber didn't ask. But juggling work, school and the kids..." His grandmother's shoulders rose and fell. "It was too much. Something had to give." She smiled at him. "So I decided to give. I've had so much fun with them."

Ethan fisted his hands. "Where's their father?"

"Tony declared himself tired of being married. Abandoned her before the girls were even born, so Amber came home where she belonged." Grandma Hicks raised her eyebrow. "To the people who love her."

An unmistakable challenge gleamed in his grandmother's bright blue eyes. In her opinion, Amber wasn't the only one who needed to come home. But besides Grandma, there was no one else who loved him.

"You won't reconsider moving to Wilmington?"

She gave him the Look.

"We're not done with this conversation, Grandma."

She sniffed. "You might not be, but I am."

"Grand—"

"Don't you Grandma me." She laced her hands on top of the coverlet. "I'm Truelove born. I'm Truelove bred. And here I'll remain until I'm Truelove dead."

Exactly what he feared most.

"With the cast, you're not going to be able to take care of yourself for a while. You have to come to Wilmington with me."

"Don't assume you know what's best for me. I don't have to do anything but die and pay taxes."

He gritted his teeth. "Grandma, please. Be reasonable."

"You're the one being unreasonable." She stuck her nose in the air. "You've seen me. I'll mend. Put your conscience at ease. I have plenty of friends who will look out for me during my recovery. You're under no obligation to stay. Feel free to get on that death-mobile of yours and head for the surf."

He tightened his jaw. "You're kicking me out? Out of town and your life?"

The lines in her face deepened. "No, honey. I told you when your dad left and then your mom remarried—we're lifers, you and me. Together forever."

"Just not in the same place at the same time, though?"

"Try to understand, Ethan." His grandmother's voice softened. "I have responsibilities here and a full life I'm not ready to abandon."

He ran his hand over his head, spiking his hair with his fingers. How could he persuade her to come with him? What could he do to change her mind?

"I'm going to pray on the situation and I suggest you do the same. Go to the house. Maybe in the morning, you'll be able to think more clearly."

He scrubbed the back of his neck. It wasn't him who needed to think more clearly. But she was right. It had been a long day for both of them. Better to let both their tempers cool before either of them said or did something from which there might be no retreat.

Ethan gave his grandmother a quick peck on the cheek. "Tomorrow," he growled. "Decisions have to be made."

Hand to her forehead, she gave him a snappy salute. "Aye aye, Captain."

"I was a marine, not navy."

She winked at him. "Good night, honey. I love you."

He sighed. "I love you, too, Grandma."

It was dark when he left the hospital. And despite being April, once the sun set behind the Blue Ridge Mountains, the night turned cool. It was only a short drive to Grandma's rambling bungalow.

Bone tired, he let himself into the house and stumbled toward his old bedroom. Not bothering to switch on a light or undress, he threw his duffel onto the floor, laid his cell on the nightstand and crawled beneath the quilt.

Hours later, he awoke to an insistent buzz from his phone on the nightstand. Groggy, he checked the incoming text message. Emergency. Call me. Now. Grandma.

Since when did ErmaJean Hicks text? Although if

anybody in her generation would learn to text, it would be his talk-to-a-signpost grandmother. Throwing off the covers, he slung his legs over the side of the bed.

He dialed her number. Surely if she'd taken a turn for the worse, a doctor or nurse would be calling him, not his grandmother. His temples throbbed.

"Grandma?" he barked into the phone. "Are you okay?"

"I'm fine."

Raking his hand over his face, he willed his pulse to settle. "You scared me to death."

"GeorgeAnne just texted me. Amber never made it home. After her night class ended, she ought to have been home by ten-thirty at the latest. GeorgeAnne fell asleep on the couch waiting for her. Or she would've contacted me sooner."

He leaned forward, the cell tucked between his shoulder and his ear. "Shouldn't we call Amber's dad, Dwight?"

"Amber wouldn't thank us for involving him. There's other stuff going on I haven't had time to share with you."

"What about calling the sheriff's office?"

"She'd be mortified if I brought the police into this. She's probably in the school parking lot trying to get that old clunker of hers started."

"All night?" His voice rose. "What if she's stranded on some deserted mountain road?"

Suppose her brakes had failed? His gut seized. The stretch of highway between the campus and town was notorious for its switchbacks and sheer drop-offs.

But it would do no good to mention that. His grandmother was worried enough already.

"I—I shouldn't have bothered you." Her voice quavered. "But GeorgeAnne and I thought it might be better if it was you who went looking."

"You did the right thing, Grandma." His bare feet hit the floor with a thud. "I'm heading out now."

His grandmother emitted an audible sigh. "Thank you, Ethan. This may change your plans for tomorrow."

"It's already tomorrow."

"The girls have already lost one parent, Ethan. You—you know what that's like."

He did know. Phone pressed against his ear, he hurriedly dressed. "Don't worry. I'm on it. I won't stop looking until I find Amber and bring her home."

But what if something unthinkable had happened to Amber?

Within minutes, he clambered aboard his motorbike. Darkness still hovered like an oppressive blanket over the ridge. Heading away from town, there were no streetlights on the isolated mountain pass. He felt as cut off as the stars shimmering dully in the fading night sky.

As much as he dared, he accelerated around the winding curves. It would do no one any good if he wrecked. It'd be daylight soon. If he didn't find Amber at the college, he'd retrace the country road. But what should he look for?

Broken branches? A damaged railing? Signs that a vehicle had plunged into a chasm.

Don't go there.

Gripping the handlebars of the bike, his knuckles turned white. As he pressed on, wisps of light streaked the horizon.

And like a film reel, those carefree, happy days in high school replayed in his mind. The Fabulous Four—Matt, Amber, Amber's best friend, Callie, and himself. The summer rafting expeditions. Football games.

Yet one image dominated his memories. A seemingly insignificant moment. A beautiful spring day. Amber and Callie had been sixteen. The four of them had hiked to a nearby meadow for a picnic.

Birdsong had called Matt and Callie away toward the gurgling melody of the fast-flowing river. Lounging at the foot of a tree, at the sound of Amber's laugh he'd glanced up. In the grass on the edge of the quilt, she'd found a blue jay feather, its hue not dissimilar to the shade of her eyes.

Sunlight streamed around her, lightening her hair. Causing it to glow. Tucking the feather behind his ear, she'd smiled at him.

And that was what he remembered when he thought of Amber—sunshine, warmth and a sense of well-being. Happiness…

"Where are you, Amber?" he whispered. "What's happened to you?" The wind tore his words away.

But he knew. Same as what happened to him. Life had changed his sunshine girl into a woman he barely recognized.

Heart pounding, he veered into the college campus. *Please let her be okay. Please let her—*

Under the security light in the parking lot, he spotted what qualified as an old clunker.

Veering into the empty space alongside the lone vehicle, he hopped off his bike. He dashed over. The glare of the streetlight silhouetted a single figure inside the car.

He tried the handle. Locked. "Amber?" He pressed his face to the window.

Was she okay? Leaning against the headrest, she appeared asleep, but frightened by her stillness, he rapped on the glass.

Bolting upright, her arms flailed. She grabbed for the steering wheel.

"Can you hear me, Amber?"

She whipped around at the sound of his voice. Forehead furrowed, she shrank into the seat. He was disconcerted by the stark fear in her eyes.

Ah. The helmet. Ripping it off, he held it under his arm and backed off a step. "It's me."

Recognition dawned in those beautiful eyes of hers. "Ethan?" Her breath fogged the window. "What are you—"

He motioned.

Springing the lock, she thrust open the door. "Where am I?" Gulping, she glanced around.

Disliking looming over her, he crouched in the opening, afraid to touch her. Afraid to further startle her.

Her gaze darted from the darkened building to his motorcycle. Checking her wristwatch, she sucked in a breath. Panic flitted across her face. "I'm supposed to be at the Jar. The girls—"

"GeorgeAnne's with them. She and Grandma sent me to find you."

Her lower lip quivered. "I spent the entire night in my car?" Tears like dewdrops trembled on the edges of her lashes. "My girls must be so worried. So—"

"Slow down, Amber. They were asleep when Grandma called. They probably don't even know you aren't there."

"I was supposed to take the girls to Before School Care. I'm already late. I can't afford to lose this job…"

The desperation in her voice hit him like a blow to the chest. "Do you feel unwell? Did you have car trouble?"

She shook her head. Like corn silk, her hair glistened in the glow of the streetlamp. "I remember thinking I'd just close my eyes for a second—" She reached for the key chain dangling from the ignition.

Amber cranked the key, but the motor didn't turn over.

Rising, his knees creaked. "Turn on the cab light."

"Why?" But she flicked the switch on the domed light above her head.

Nothing happened. Just as he'd suspected.

"Maybe the bulb's burned out."

He rested his forearms against the door frame. "The battery's dead, Amber."

She tried starting the engine again. "It can't be dead. Give me a minute."

He shook his head. "The car's dead. Come on, I'll take you back to Truelove."

"I don't need your help. I can drive myself."

So stubborn. So obstinate. So aggravating.

Wait, hadn't Grandma said the same about him yesterday?

"Your car will have to be towed."

Her mouth went mulish. "I can't afford a tow truck." Then her shoulders sagged. "I've failed my children so much."

Bands of pink and gold brightened the sky.

"Give yourself a break, Amber. Working full-time, going to school at night. Single parenting. Something's got to give. You aren't Superwoman."

She stared through the windshield. "I'm not a super anything."

It absolutely killed him to hear her talk like that about herself. And reverting to form, when he couldn't fix something, he got angry.

"Get out of the car. I'm taking you home."

Her expression turned furious. "You don't get to tell me what to do, Ethan Green."

Widening his stance, he crossed his arms over his jacket. "Unless you want to miss your entire shift, I suggest you chuck that boulder-sized pride of yours and get on my Harley."

If looks could kill, he figured he would be struck stone dead on the spot.

"Suit yourself—sit here all day…" Feigning nonchalance, he raised his palms. "Or after I drop you off, I could install a new battery for you."

Amber jutted her chin. "Seeing as you are so eager to leave Truelove in the dust *again*, I couldn't ask you to do that for me."

"You're not asking. I'm offering. It's what friends do for each other." He cocked his head. "We've always been friends. Or had you forgotten?"

She gave him an inscrutable look. "I haven't forgotten."

Guilt pricked his conscience. He should have kept in touch. But he'd been determined to put his own bad memories behind him when he joined the Corps. Amber had been unintentionally jettisoned, too. Collateral damage.

Yet if there was anything from his broken childhood he would've wanted to carry with him, it would have been those wonderful times with the Flemings. They'd been good to him. Embracing him like one of their own.

When he'd been seven, his dad had abandoned him and his mom, and they'd lived with his grandparents. Later when his mom moved away into a new life, Grandma had offered to let him stay with her so he could finish high school with his friends. It was a pattern with his grandmother. Maybe that was why she was trying so hard to help Amber finish her schooling.

"Grandma's still at the hospital. I can't leave today, anyway. A few more days in Truelove won't matter."

The corners of Amber's lovely mouth pulled downward. "I guess it won't."

He stepped aside. "Grandma will relish having another chance to give me what for."

Slinging a backpack over her shoulder, Amber eased out of the car. "Your grandmother adores you. That's why she's so tough on you."

He took the backpack. "So we're good? You and me?"

Their gazes locked. Something tightened in his chest when she didn't answer right away. Finally—

Her lashes lowered, sweeping her cheeks. "We're good, Ethan."

But clicking the fob to lock the car, she gave him a nice view of her back.

To say that having fallen asleep in her car was an embarrassment would have been an understatement. That Ethan had been the one to find her was a complete humiliation.

And to have to depend on him—on any man—was merely the latest tier on a cake of mortification she'd been building since Tony proved her father right about everything.

In two months, she would earn her nursing license. Over the last year and a half, she'd consoled herself with the thought of getting a good-paying job. Showing her father how wrong he'd been. Standing on her own two feet.

But everything had been contingent on finishing nursing school. After yesterday, it was a goal that had dissipated as quickly as morning mist over the mountains.

Amber shot a surreptitious look at Ethan typing into his cell. Her girls depended on her to make a better life for them. She couldn't—wouldn't—let them down. No matter what it took. No matter if, in the process, she half killed herself.

She shuddered, recalling other late nights over the winter where she'd almost fallen asleep at the wheel. Driving the treacherous mountain roads, oftentimes through whiteout conditions. Several times she'd come close to losing control of the car. And then what would've become of her children?

Putting away his phone, Ethan stowed her backpack in a compartment on the motorcycle. "I texted Grandma. Explained what happened. Told her we're on our way to Truelove."

Amber nodded.

"I'm glad you have a jacket." He climbed on the bike. "Doesn't feel like spring yet."

Strapping on the extra helmet, she took the seat behind him. "I'm ready."

"Hold on," he yelled above the roar of the engine.

Biting her lip, she locked her arms around his waist. And they were off.

Last fall, after Callie and Jake got married, Miss ErmaJean had offered—insisted—on taking the girls to school each morning while Amber reported for the early-morning shift at the diner. ErmaJean had also cared for Lucy and Stella the two evenings a week Amber attended class. And each weekend during Amber's clinicals.

But Miss ErmaJean was an old woman. Lucy and Stella weren't her responsibility. If anything ever happened to Amber, her brother, Matt, would be their guardian. Yet he was often unreachable for weeks at a time on a classified mission. As for her father?

The glossy, evergreen leaves of rhododendron flashed by on either side of the mountain road. Wind whipped her hair across her eyes. The early-morning chill stung her cheeks.

Her father had never met the twins.

She pressed her face into Ethan's buttery soft, brown leather jacket.

You make your bed hard, you can lie in it. That's what her father had said when she told him she was going to marry Tony. It had been the biggest mistake of her life. And lying in that hard bed was what she'd been doing ever since.

At the crossroads on the outskirts of Truelove, Ethan slowed. The decibel level of the motor lessened measurably. "Where do you live?"

When he saw where she was living, it would be the final indignity.

Following her directions, he turned onto a secondary road. Midway up the mountain at the third gravel driveway, he pulled in beside Miss GeorgeAnne's sturdy pickup truck and cut the engine.

He did a quick scan of her dilapidated trailer.

She clenched her teeth. "This is all I can afford."

"I didn't say anything."

Letting go of him, she stepped onto the ground. "You didn't have to say anything."

To her dismay, he hopped off, too. Retrieving her pack, he followed her to the porch steps.

She reached for her backpack. "You don't have to—"

The railing wobbled under his hand. He looked at her again. And refused to surrender the pack.

She chewed her lip, wishing the yard would swallow her. But no chance of that. She headed up the steps to the door. The porch landing shook under his weight, and he muttered something under his breath.

GeorgeAnne flung open the door. "I was so worried.

I didn't know what else to do but get ErmaJean to call Ethan. I figured you wouldn't want me to call your—"

"It's okay, Miss GeorgeAnne. I'm so, so sorry you had to spend the night here with the girls."

GeorgeAnne's gaze flicked to Ethan. "Staying with Lucy and Stella is no trouble."

Ducking his head, he stepped inside the low-ceilinged living room.

Amber did a slow three-sixty on the worn carpet. "Where are the girls?"

GeorgeAnne patted her shoulder. "Haven't stirred since I put them to bed last night. They'll be awake soon and find their mommy waiting to wish them a good day at school."

Amber pinched her lips together. "The manager at the Jar isn't the most understanding of men. He's probably sacked me."

GeorgeAnne pushed her wire-frame glasses higher on the bridge of her nose. "The girls and I put an emergency plan in motion until you can get to the diner."

Ethan leaned the long length of himself against a kitchen cabinet. "You and the twins put a plan in motion?"

Amber prayed the cabinet didn't give way under him. Most things in the trailer were held together with little more than duct tape and prayer. "Miss GeorgeAnne means *her* girls."

His eyes widened. "The matchmakers?"

GeorgeAnne looked down her long nose at him. "We had a conference call this morning about Amber's situation."

"A conference call." He eyed the older lady. "Seriously?"

"Your generation does not have the market cornered

on technology or intelligence. Don't forget, it was my generation that sent a man to the moon." She jabbed her finger in his chest.

He winced. "Ow, Miss GeorgeAnne—"

"And invented computers, which your generation can't pull your head out from." She jabbed him again. "Did the Marines teach you nothing? Stand up straight, young man."

He straightened. "Yes, ma'am."

Pushing him aside, GeorgeAnne opened the cabinet. "IdaLee has the diner under control. She said not to rush. To get there when you can."

Amber's mouth fell open.

GeorgeAnne removed several coffee mugs from the cabinet. "Her nephew-in-law is the manager."

Amber slow-blinked. Twice. "Miss IdaLee is waitressing in my place at the Jar this morning?"

Ethan hooted. "I'd pay good money to see that."

GeorgeAnne shot him a reproving glance, but her lips twitched. "You could, except ErmaJean texted she wants to talk with you ASAP. I'll take Amber to work." His grandmother's lifelong friend lumbered over to the coffee maker sitting on the chipped linoleum countertop. "After she has a chance to shower and change clothes."

Amber frowned. "I should just go. Now."

"I believe we've both received our marching orders." Ethan smirked. "Best not cross Miss GeorgeAnne and the girls."

GeorgeAnne shooed Amber out of the kitchen. "I'll get the twins to school this morning, too."

"I can't thank you enough for everything you've…" Amber worried her lip with her teeth. "I promise nothing like this will ever happen again, Miss GeorgeAnne. I'm so sorry—"

"Stop with the apologizing," Ethan growled.

Her eyes welled. Angry with herself, she swiped at the tears with her hand.

Ethan's face fell. "I didn't mean to…"

"It's okay." She was going to lose it in front of him if she didn't put distance between them right this minute. "It's just the both of you—your kindness…"

Before she fractured completely, she fled down the hall to her bedroom. Shutting the door on the man who'd once been her fondest adolescent dream. Closing her eyes, she leaned against the door. Steeling herself to what could never be.

Perhaps the saddest words of all.

Chapter Three

After Amber disappeared down the hall, Ethan rounded on GeorgeAnne. "Why does kindness make Amber cry?"

"Because she isn't used to it." The older woman's face shadowed. "She's forgotten what it's like."

"I can't believe her father would let her live here. Why didn't Grandma Hicks want to call Dwight?"

"Dwight is a proud man. Too proud to admit he made a mistake." GeorgeAnne opened a cabinet over the coffee maker. "They've been estranged ever since Amber ran off to marry that no-good rafting guide."

"What about her friends?"

"Callie has helped—we all have—as much as Amber will let us." GeorgeAnne pointed to a coffee can higher than her reach.

Ethan pulled the can off the shelf and handed it to his grandmother's dear friend. "Dwight's not the only one too proud to admit when he's wrong."

GeorgeAnne scooped coffee grounds into the filter basket. "Amber knows she made a terrible mistake when she married Tony."

Despite the exterior of the trailer, Amber's kitchen was spotless. He could've eaten off those shiny floors of hers. The interior was immaculate if threadbare. There were no photos of the jerk who deserted Amber and left her to raise his kids alone.

"Neither Dwight nor Amber will budge an inch." GeorgeAnne filled the glass carafe with water from the kitchen faucet. "Nor ask the other for forgiveness."

Ethan grunted. "Leaving both of them miserable."

"That's not the worst of it." GeorgeAnne's mouth pursed. "What this is doing to the twins is—"

At the other end of the trailer, a door banged.

GeorgeAnne's face shifted into a semblance of what for other people constituted a smile. "Speaking of..."

And not unlike a herd of elephants, the two small girls, their blond hair in pigtails, stampeded across the living room.

"Sounds like there ought to be at least a dozen of them, doesn't there?" GeorgeAnne gave him a wry look. "Sunrise to bedtime, those girls are full of energy."

Barefoot, they bounded toward the kitchen in their Disney princess pajamas. Catching sight of him, the twins skidded to a stop.

Lucy—the bolder of the two—sidled closer. "Hey, Efan."

Stella, the aloof one, glowered at him. GeorgeAnne bustled around the tiny kitchen, dishing out cereal. The milk jug wobbled in Stella's grasp. In the nick of time, he grabbed hold and steadied the jug. Tilting it slightly, he helped her pour the milk over her cereal.

"Thank you," she whispered, not raising her eyes from the bowl.

Across the table, Lucy smiled at him, dimples in her cheeks. And despite his resolve to remain unaffected, he found himself pulling out a chair and sitting down. "Tell me about school."

Lucy waved her spoon. "We have art today. Stehwaa's favowite. I wike when we do maf." Crunch. Crunch. Swallow. Gulp. "And…"

He grinned. "Slow down, Lucy Lou."

Mini-Amber giggled. "My name's not Woocy Woo, Efan."

"Of course it is." He angled toward the quiet twin. "And you're Stella Bella."

Lucy dissolved into giggles. "She's not Stehwaa Beh-waa."

Shooting him an unamused look, Stella continued to chew.

Amber hurried into the kitchen. "Losing your touch with the ladies, Ethan?" GeorgeAnne handed her a coffee mug, and she took a sip.

Smiling, he shrugged. "It's a tough crowd. But seriously?" He looked at Amber. "I don't know how you have the energy to do everything you do."

Amber ambled around the table, bestowing a kiss on the forehead of each girl. "It's not hard when you have two little morning glories to help you greet each day."

His cell phone vibrated in his pocket. Rising from the table, he fished it out and frowned at the text. "My grandmother. I guess I should head out."

"Bye, Efan." Lucy fluttered her fingers. "Make it a good one."

He laughed. "You, too, kid." He ruffled her hair.

Amber bit back a smile. "That's what I tell the girls every morning."

"Goodbye, Stella Bella." Strangely reluctant to leave, for the briefest of seconds he laid his hand on her small, delicate shoulder. "Have a good day at school." And he considered it a triumph when she didn't instantly shrug him off.

It occurred to him he might not see the girls or Amber ever again. Not if he could convince his grandmother to leave town when she was released from the hospital. Suddenly, it seemed as if the oxygen in the trailer had vanished.

Amber got up from the table. "Let me walk you out."

"I guess this is goodbye, then," he rasped.

Stumbling to the porch, he grabbed the railing for support. That was a mistake that nearly pitched him over the side to the ground below.

What kind of bum of a landlord would leave a young mother and two little girls to live in such conditions? An entire punch list of items needed to be tackled at the trailer. His stomach knotted. But he wouldn't be here to make sure everything was properly fixed.

"I can't thank you enough for coming to my rescue, Ethan." She wrapped her light gray cardigan around herself against the crisp chill of the April morning. "It—it was good to see you again."

Never seeing *them* again unsettled him in a way he wouldn't have previously believed possible. He had only the briefest acquaintance with the twins. But already, they'd somehow managed to entangle themselves in his heart.

Kind of like…kudzu. Or morning glories.

And then there was Amber.

His chest heaved. "It was great seeing you, too, Amber. And meeting your girls."

"Thank you for making the effort to reach out to Stella." She nudged her chin toward the trailer. "Lucy is so outgoing, people naturally respond to her, but her sister—"

"Just because she's quiet and reserved, Stella should never be consigned to the shadows." He jutted his jaw.

"You, Lucy and Stella deserve only sunshine, blue skies and happy days."

"Lucy and Stella, yes."

The bone-weary defeat in Amber's eyes almost undid him.

She squared her too-thin shoulders. "Please tell your grandmother goodbye for me and the girls. It will break their hearts when I tell them she's moving away, but I understand, Ethan, that you have to do what you think is best."

Her blue eyes pooling, she hastily stepped inside the trailer. Leaving him standing on the stoop, staring at the closed door. Questioning if he really knew what was best for his grandmother. Best for himself.

Best for anyone.

Ethan no sooner walked into his grandmother's hospital room than he realized Grandma Hicks was loaded for bear. And he, apparently, was the bear.

"Before I can be released, the nurse said she has to go over instructions for at-home care with you. Or a responsible adult." His grandmother sniffed, as if the likelihood of him proving a responsible adult was slim to none. "But we need to talk first."

Hadn't he said as much last night?

"GeorgeAnne, IdaLee and I have been thinking on my dilemma."

Uh-oh. Here comes trouble.

"How about we make a deal?" His grandmother's blue-denim eyes flashed. "I know how you love a good deal."

Ethan narrowed his gaze. "What kind of deal, Grandma?"

"I promised Amber I'd take care of the girls until she graduates from nursing school in two months."

He blew out a breath, praying for patience. "You're going to be in this cast for weeks. Be reasonable. You can't possibly take care of two little girls."

She slitted her eyes at him. "But *you* can."

He blinked. Twice. "You want me to nanny two little girls?"

That settled it—Grandma Hicks had officially lost touch with reality.

"Don't tell me a big, strong marine like you is scared of a couple of four-year-olds?"

"I'd be outnumbered," he grunted.

"You're a chicken."

"I am not a—" He pressed his lips together. "Besides, Amber would never allow her children to be…" He made a face. "To be nannied by me. What do I know about kids?"

"You were a kid once." Grandma Hicks quirked her eyebrow. "Some would say you've never grown up." She gave him a calculated smile. "But there's nothing like a kid—or two—to mature a man."

"I don't know anything about girls."

She raised her eyes to the ceiling. "If that's not the truth…"

"Grandma," he growled.

"You want me to give up my entire life and come live with you? My friends. My house. My church. My business." Her gaze locked with his. "I have a proposition for you. Stay with me in Truelove for two months while I finish my convalescence. Take care of the girls until Amber graduates, and then I'll go with you to Wilmington."

He frowned. "You'll actually sell the house? Pull up stakes? Move away? Without protest?"

"I will." Grandma Hicks lifted her chin. "Do we have ourselves a bargain, Ethan?"

He stared at her. His plan to have Grandma live where he could watch over her lay almost within his grasp. They could spend more time together.

Ice cream. Sand. Ocean waves.

And all he had to do was to consent to this unorthodox arrangement?

It troubled him how he'd left things with Amber. The crushing burden Amber shouldered alone weighed him down. He knew a lot about being alone.

"Amber will never agree, Grandma."

Her eyebrow rose. "If you put your mind to it, I'm sure you'll convince her. She values your insight."

Since when? But he couldn't afford to relinquish the prospect of getting Grandma to the coast.

"If I agree to this… And it's a big if…"

His grandmother's blue-veined hand smoothed the coverlet. "It will work out, Ethan. Trust me."

Those words coming from Grandma Hicks's mouth sent a shaft of terror into his heart, only slightly less frightening than the thought of being in charge of four-year-old twins.

Key word—*slightly.*

Aghast, Amber stared at ErmaJean. "You want me to leave my girls with Ethan?"

The older lady sat in a wheelchair beside the hospital bed, awaiting a physical therapy evaluation. She'd texted Amber late that morning, asking her to visit the hospital before collecting the girls from school.

Ethan had not only installed a new battery into her car, but also managed to leave it parked at the Mason Jar, ready for her once she finished her shift.

"Don't look at me as if you think I'm crazy." Clad in a loose, baby-blue velour jogging suit, ErmaJean's neon pink leg cast stuck out from the foot piece. "It would be entirely under my supervision, of course. And I think there would be lots of advantages to this short-term arrangement."

Amber shook her head. "Ethan Green? We're talking about your grandson?"

His grandmother rested her hands on the armrests. "You must finish nursing training, and I promised to take care of the girls."

Amber threw out her hands. "I don't expect you to take care of the girls after you broke your leg."

"I keep my promises, Amber."

"But, Miss ErmaJean—"

"How will you finish your studies if someone doesn't take care of the girls for you?"

She wouldn't be able to finish. In her mind, she'd already composed the email, tendering her withdrawal from the program.

ErmaJean folded her hands in her lap. "Do you have anyone else to take care of the girls?"

Spring was *the* big season for Callie's fledgling photography career. She wouldn't derail her best friend's dreams.

Biting her lip, Amber looked out the window over the parking lot. "No."

"Are you concerned that Ethan would harm or allow harm to come to the girls?"

Her gaze snapped to ErmaJean. "Of course not. Ethan would never hurt the girls."

Ethan Green might be terminally charming and perennially rootless, but she'd spent enough time with her brother's best friend to know he had a good heart.

"So you think he's just not responsible enough to be entrusted with their care?"

"No offense, Miss ErmaJean, but your grandson isn't exactly the poster boy for stick-to-it-iveness."

"I'm praying he'll rise as the occasion demands. I've always believed there were unplumbed depths to him." ErmaJean squared her shoulders. "But I would never hazard Lucy's and Stella's well-being if you're opposed to Ethan twin-sitting them. A mother's instincts must always be heeded."

Problem was—it wasn't so much Amber's motherly instincts that gave her pause as it was the younger Amber who lived somewhere still inside her heart. The one who'd followed her brother and Ethan everywhere. The girl who believed Ethan hung the moon and then some.

Though after his father deserted him, the sweet boy she'd known had morphed into a cocky heartbreaker. In high school, he'd gone through a string of girlfriends. Then Mr. Love 'Em and Leave 'Em had walked away from Truelove as soon as he'd turned eighteen.

She sighed. "It's not Ethan I distrust."

ErmaJean's eyes flickered. "What was that, Amber dear?"

"Nothing." Amber raised her chin. "I don't object to Ethan looking after my girls. But Ethan told me you would be finishing your convalescence in Wilmington."

"I prevailed upon Ethan to reconsider. That I would recover best at home. He agreed to stay in Truelove for a while."

Ethan staying in Truelove? The idea sent a funny little pang into her heart. Biting her lip, she reminded herself Miss ErmaJean had said "a while." A while meant only a temporary stay.

"So you won't be moving to the beach?"

ErmaJean's gaze dropped. "If my recovery goes as

well as I hope, I'm believing relocating won't be necessary."

Amber exhaled. "You have no idea how thrilled I am to hear you're not leaving." She clasped the woman's hand. "I'd feel so lost without you—I mean, the girls would miss having you in their lives."

"It's okay to need people, honey."

She looked away. "That hasn't worked out so well for me, Miss ErmaJean."

"You and Ethan are more alike than you know."

"I never understood what Ethan has against Truelove. Sure, it's a sleepy, laid-back kind of town. But that's part of its charm."

ErmaJean brushed her hand across the shiny grain of the velour jacket. "He connects Truelove with his father's abandonment. A place of broken endings. He and my daughter are still in touch, but after her remarriage, he never felt welcome in her new life. He associates Truelove with his feelings of being cast aside."

Perhaps she and Ethan *were* more alike than she'd realized. She was still working through the feelings of inadequacy and self-doubt Tony's casting aside triggered within her.

"Why, then, would Ethan even consider staying on and twin-sitting?"

ErmaJean pursed her lips. "Perhaps in his heart, he's looking for a second chance."

"At what?"

"Redemption. For a new beginning." ErmaJean folded her hands. "There's another advantage to this arrangement. For the girls."

"What possible advantage to Ethan's care could there be for Lucy and Stella?"

ErmaJean fixed her gaze on Amber. "The girls don't spend much time with men, Amber."

She stiffened. "They spend time with Maisie's dad, Jake."

"Not that much. The girls need a strong male role model." ErmaJean's eyes softened. "Unless you think your dad might—"

"My father isn't likely to ever be in their lives."

Amber tucked a stray tendril behind her ear. She was aware of the statistics. Girls who grew up without a father were far more likely to experiment with a host of unhealthy life choices.

"Ethan is hardly father material, Miss ErmaJean."

"How about we let him try? Who knows? He might surprise you." ErmaJean's too-observant gaze probed Amber's features. "Or is that what you're really afraid of?"

Was she afraid of Ethan? Or just afraid of herself? This arrangement would mean the girls wouldn't be the only ones spending time with him over the next two months. She'd see him, talk to him—every time she dropped off the twins and picked them up.

Panic bubbled inside her chest. "Suppose the girls get too attached. When he leaves, they could be devastated."

"Why don't we cross that bridge when we come to it?" ErmaJean rested her shoulder blades against the chair. "Don't borrow trouble. Get through school, and let the good Lord work out the rest of the details."

"What if the girls don't like him?"

ErmaJean laughed. "When have girls ever not liked my grandson?"

Ain't that the truth. As in, never. Amber gnashed her teeth.

ErmaJean waved her hand. "Lucy already likes Ethan. And Stella doesn't dislike him."

Her slower-to-warm child had trust issues. Amber winced. Just like Stella's mother.

"I have no doubt, in her own time, Stella will be no more able to resist Ethan's charm than the rest of us."

Amber had a sinking feeling ErmaJean was right. Seeing him in the hospital lobby yesterday had brought back so many feelings. Feelings she believed she'd forever buried in the graveyard of her heart.

"What do you say?" ErmaJean opened her hands. "Shall we give it a go, Amber dear?"

Spent of objections, Amber took a deep breath. "We have a deal. But if either of the girls are unhappy... Or their presence hampers your recovery... Or—"

"Or pigs fly." ErmaJean smiled.

Amber didn't smile. "Or Ethan decides to bail."

ErmaJean inclined her head. "Then we'll reevaluate the terms of our arrangement. Agreed?"

"Agreed." Amber swallowed. "For now."

What choice did she have? None, if she truly wanted to finish school and make a better life for her children.

ErmaJean plucked her cell phone out of her pocket. "I'll give Ethan the good news. And you two can work out the details."

Would this be good news to Ethan?

Soon after, the physical therapist bustled into the room, and Amber said goodbye. Heading down the corridor, she had the disquieting thought she'd just agreed to something irrevocable. Had she set up not only herself but her children, too, for more pain?

This would not turn out well. This could not turn out well at all. Where she and Ethan were concerned, it never had.

Chapter Four

It had taken Ethan most of the morning to put a new battery in Amber's car. At his grandmother's suggestion, he'd called and asked Callie's father, Nash Jackson, to give him a hand in shuttling Amber's vehicle to Truelove. Ethan had been afraid the fiftysomething apple grower might refuse to ride with him on the Harley. But he needn't have worried—the young-at-heart grandfather considered it a hoot.

"Folks who think they're too old to enjoy an adventure might as well call it a day." A twinkle gleamed in Nash's eye. "As for me? I aim to embrace each and every opportunity that comes my way."

Ethan wasn't sure what he meant by that, but he conceded the years had been kind to Callie's father. He hoped to be as fit and happy as Nash when he was that age. Although happiness had somehow always eluded him, always seeming just out of his reach.

Back at the house, in the broad light of day, he concluded adaptations would have to be made to the old family home to accommodate his grandmother's injury. Since neither the Harley nor Grandma's sedan was suitable for the task, he arranged for the local home building supply store to deliver lumber that afternoon.

He enjoyed rummaging through his grandpa's old workshop behind the house for the tools he'd need in making the house more accessible.

The next morning, he got an early start. With his grandmother scheduled to be released late in the afternoon, he had to get the project finished. The day promised to be crazy busy, and he worked steadily through the morning hours.

Only when his stomach growled did he realize it was already lunchtime. Screwing the bolt in place, he surveyed his handiwork. He shook the handrail. Unlike Amber's flimsy porch, the ramp was sturdy enough to get his grandmother in and out of the house safely.

If only every problem was as easily fixed. The nurse had gone over his grandmother's recovery plan with him yesterday. He would need to bring his grandmother to physical therapy sessions and follow-up appointments with several medical professionals.

The nurse had carefully explained what tasks he'd have to oversee regarding his grandmother's care. Issues neither he—nor he suspected Grandma—had considered in making the decision to finish her recovery at home and not in a rehab facility. The nurse had raised delicate questions regarding personal hygiene and privacy.

With his hand, he worked the kinks out of his neck. The last few boards could wait until after he ate. He could do with a break and a hearty meal.

Brushing the sawdust from his jeans, he got on the Harley and headed to the Mason Jar. Kill two birds with one stone. He'd fill his belly and get the details from Amber about twin-sitting.

After all these years, it was almost surreal being back

in town. But the more things changed, the more they stayed the same.

He parked outside the diner, stowing his helmet. And he took his first good look around the hometown he'd left behind without a second glance. Believing he'd never return to this Podunk mountain town.

Yet here he was. But wiser, or so he liked to think. In the decade since high school, more than once life had taken him to the proverbial woodshed

Not much appeared to have changed in Truelove, North Carolina. Same old town square. The shops on Main. The river that bent around the town like a horse-shoe. And the perpetual smoky mist off the surrounding Blue Ridge.

Old mountains. Almost as old as Ethan felt after surviving four tours in a war zone. Though not as jagged as the mountains where he'd hunted terrorists—and been hunted in return. The sharp peaks of the Appalachians were blunted, worn away by time.

Kind of like him.

The parking lot was filled with the late-lunch crowd. And just beyond, he could see the sign on the edge of town that proclaimed Truelove, Where True Love Awaits.

Only thing that waited for him when he finished his deployment had been the terse Dear Ethan letter his girl-friend, Kelly, left him.

Lesson learned the hard way. His usual modus ope-randi, Grandma Hicks would've said. But he was finished with romantic relationships. No more putting his heart out there for target practice.

No sirree, Bob. Or whatever the next pretty face's name might be. Stick a fork in him—he was done with women. Who needs 'em!

He took a cautious, exploratory breath of the pine-scented mountain air. A cleansing breath.

Weird, how suddenly dear and familiar it seemed. Like a lovely dream barely recalled. Like home?

But anything was better than the dust—always the dust—and the dry scorching heat that passed for spring in Afghanistan. Only person missing from the Fab Four now was Amber's brother, Matt.

Ethan didn't have many friends. But those he had, he cherished. None more so than his best friend since childhood. His coconspirator in the up-to-no-good department, Grandma Hicks used to say. She'd also had plenty to say about some of his more unfortunate, recent life choices.

The bell jangled above the door as he stepped into the café. The aroma of fried eggs and the yeasty smell of biscuits floated past his nostrils. His stomach rumbled again, reminding him it had been a long time since the doughnuts Nash brought by that morning.

Heads turned at the sound of the bell. Conversation momentarily ground to a halt. But with no display of recognition for the stranger in their midst, the regulars soon returned to fueling their bellies.

It felt strange, thinking of himself—who'd grown up here—as a stranger. No doubt Truelove had written him off as a lost cause years ago. Yet here he was. Like a bad penny.

The diner was jam-packed. Waitresses in jeans and long-sleeved Mason Jar T-shirts scurried from table to table. No sign of Amber.

He recognized most of the people from his boyhood. But putting a name to their faces was another thing entirely. He'd been gone too long.

When two men in the blue overalls of the local auto

repair shop exited a booth, Ethan slid in after them. He ran a practiced eye over the crowd. Force of habit. Always good to know from which direction the next attack might come.

But there was only the Jar's usual clientele—farmers, ranchers and such. An old football compatriot waved at him from a stool at the counter. And at the table against the far wall underneath the town bulletin board—

Ethan ducked his head, lying low in the booth. Praying none of his grandma's posse spotted him. Prayer was not something he'd done much since shaking the North Carolina mountain dirt off his feet.

Too late. Spotting him, GeorgeAnne gave him the evil eye. IdaLee Moore pushed back her chair. And two of the infamous nosy musketeers headed his way. He hunkered lower in the booth. *Keep walking... Keep walking...*

"What did I tell you yesterday about that slouching?" Her iron-gray hair like a helmet, GeorgeAnne widened her stance beside the booth. "I'd think a decorated marine like yourself would've learned to sit straight."

Older than his grandma or GeorgeAnne, IdaLee sniffed. "Never could get him to sit straight in the classroom, either."

At the sound of her voice, like a Pavlovian-trained dog, he sat up straighter in his seat.

Miss GeorgeAnne crossed her arms. "Have you brought your grandmother home from the hospital yet, young man?"

This was why he'd departed Truelove never to return— or so he'd hoped. Everyone felt it their duty to parent— aka micromanage—everyone else's kids.

One of many reasons why he'd champed at the bit to get away. He forcibly reminded himself he was no longer a teenager. He was a grown man. A war veteran. He need not be intimidated by anyone, much less a bunch of—

"You forget how to talk? Let it never be said some things don't improve over time," Miss GeorgeAnne hooted.

He took a long—and deep—breath. "No, ma'am." Grandma Hicks had drummed politeness into him. The Marines had mortared in respect. "I haven't forgotten how to talk."

Miss IdaLee's patrician face wrinkled like a well-worn map. "More's the shame. You've always been trouble with a capital T."

Craning around them, he scoped out the diner again, hoping for a glimpse of Amber. "Grandma won't be re-leased until this afternoon. Amber and I need to work out my twin-sitting responsibilities."

"Lucy and Stella?" Miss GeorgeAnne's slitted gray eyes had taken on an ominous gleam. "When ErmaJean first floated the idea by me, I never believed you'd agree. So you *are* going to take on the twins?"

Wary as a turkey before Thanksgiving, he nodded... slowly.

The old women gave each other a significant look.

Diminutive IdaLee tilted her head, the hairs in her schoolteacher bun white with age. "Well, well, well. You and Amber will see a lot of each other over the next few months."

Too late he remembered the Double Name Club's favorite civic activity.

He gulped. But nobody in their right mind would ever willingly pair Amber with a rebellious drifter like him. His previous reputation *was* well deserved.

But GeorgeAnne's face cleared. "Amber's in the kitchen plating an order." The no-nonsense owner of the local hardware store motioned toward the swinging door behind the counter. "She'll be out in a minute."

Feeling not unlike he'd received a presidential pardon, he swiped a distracted hand across the top of his head.

"And get that hair cut." IdaLee wagged her gnarled finger. "Before you give your grandmother a heart attack," she growled as a final parting shot.

Heads high, the matchmakers marched toward the door.

Limp with relief at somehow emerging relatively intact, he let his head fall against the booth. Not unlike his feelings after surviving that last street battle in Kandahar.

At a whoosh of air, he lifted his gaze. And his stomach bottomed out when Amber, laden with an enormous serving tray, hurried out of the kitchen. Delivering the order to a nearby table, she quickly unloaded the plates.

She turned in his direction. And her lovely sky-blue eyes widened, locking on to his. His heart did a strange sort of flip-flop.

Because indeed, somehow the more things changed, the more they stayed the same.

At the sight of Ethan, her heart jolted. Like a bolt of lightning sizzling her brain. Was he waiting for her? That would be a change. He couldn't be waiting for her.

Yet the way he looked at her... Nerves suddenly assailed Amber. Of all the booths in the café, why did he have to be in one of hers? She'd have to go over and talk to him. Take his order.

She'd tossed and turned all night after agreeing to ErmaJean's surprising proposal. Finally in the wee hours of the morning, she'd come to the inescapable conclusion she needed to decline. One thing she still couldn't fathom—why Ethan would agree to such a ridiculous plan.

Unless... What if he felt sorry for her? Something twisted like a knife in her gut. Had he agreed because he pitied her?

Maybe it was better that he was here at the Jar.

She could tell him in person she'd decided to refuse his grandmother's offer. In full view of the dining public with the people who knew her best. People who'd seen her at her worst. That would keep her grounded about who she really was.

The stupid, grief-stricken girl who ran away with a loser and returned divorced with infant twins. Ashamed of her past, a woman whose only future consisted of doing right by her daughters.

Amber tucked the empty tray underneath her arm. She should also take care to remember who Ethan Green was—a handsome, charming, marginally reckless, rolling stone.

Why was he staring at her? Self-conscious, she smoothed her hand over her jeans. The strain of the years had taken their toll. She no longer resembled the idealistic young girl he'd once known.

Stop stalling.

Clamping the tray against her side, she forced her feet to move toward him. She hoped he'd learned to tip better since high school. But big spender or not, a single mom couldn't afford to lose even a meager gratuity.

Lips pursed, she crossed the last few yards dividing them. "Let me clear the table for you."

Balancing the tray on the corner of the sticky laminate tabletop with her hip, she loaded the dirty glasses.

Maybe if she kept her head down, didn't look too closely at him, her pulse would—

"Amber."

Reaching for a crumpled, discarded napkin, her hand

quivered. If he only knew what the sound of her name on his lips had always done to her. Frantically, she snatched at anything she could lay her hands on—dirty plates, more napkins. The utensils.

His hand on hers stilled her frenzied attempts at normalcy. Her gaze flitted to his face. That was a mistake. Cold sweat broke out on her forehead.

Ethan's blond hair no longer resembled the close-cropped military cut in the pictures on Miss ErmaJean's mantel. Once again, he wore his hair a tad too long for conservative local tastes. Just like in high school.

Ditto to the strong brow. Rugged features. Square lantern jaw.

Her crush had been entirely one-sided, of course. To him, she was Matt's baby sister. Ethan's little buddy—practically his sister, too.

At least he'd never guessed how she felt. Her pride spared that humiliation. And these days, pride was a hard commodity for Amber to hold on to. It was all she had. Except for her girls.

She moistened her bottom lip. "Wh-what are you doing here?" *She* blushed, but he didn't notice. He never noticed, not when it came to her.

"I'm here to see you." He grinned, and her heart dropped to her toes. "Who else, baby cakes?"

Devastatingly handsome and oh so charming.

"Me?" The word came out of her mouth with a squeak.

She flushed. *Get it together, Amber.* But Ethan Green had always reduced her to a gibbering, melted puddle of hope and unrequited feelings.

What was the matter with her? She was no longer a naive, dreamy teenager. She was a grown woman with responsibilities. She'd believed herself long past such schoolgirl palpitations.

Apparently not when it came to him.

She strove for a professional calm. "What can I get for you, Ethan?"

"Just yourself." Blinking, he reared a fraction. "I mean…"

Ethan scrubbed his palm over his face. "I want to talk about what I need to do to take care of the girls."

Her hands tightened around the edges of the tray. "Now that I've had some time to reflect, I'm thinking we should forget the whole thing."

"Wait… No." His face dropped. "Let's talk about this first, Amber."

She glanced around. "Unless you order something, the boss won't like you occupying a booth."

"Okay." Resting his shoulder blades against the blue vinyl upholstery, he gave her a half-lidded stare. "I'll have what you're having."

She hoisted the tray. "I'm not having anything. I work here."

He leaned forward, placing the coiled muscles of his forearms on the table. "Everyone gets a break."

She blew out a breath. "It's the lunch rush, Ethan. Surely you've not been away so long you've forgotten that."

His eyes flicked to the wall where a clock hung above the pass-through window. "Half an hour more, right? I can wait. We should catch up."

"Why?"

He cocked his head. "Because you always were my best girl." Again with the effortless charm. "You and Grandma. I want to hear what you've been doing with your life while I've been protecting the free world from tyranny." He grinned.

"Always so full of yourself." She rolled her eyes. "And

you know what I've been doing with my life—Lucy and Stella."

"I want to hear about your life, Amber. And we need to talk about the girls."

She narrowed her eyes at him. "Order something, Ethan."

His lips twitched. "Coffee."

"Black as your heart?" She arched her eyebrow. "That's what you used to say."

He laughed. "And it's still true."

"What else do you want for lunch?"

His strong white teeth had an almost seismic effect on her equilibrium. "Surprise me."

Ethan Green really ought to come with warning labels.

When he turned that lethal charm on her, she was as good as lost. Making her no different than any other female in Truelove. Which he knew. He'd always known. How could he not help but know?

"And give or take thirty minutes, we'll talk. Okay, Amber? I've missed talking to you."

She couldn't stop the smile from breaking out on her face. "Coffee coming right up. And your surprise lunch."

Leaning against the back of the booth, he winked. "I trust you."

Problem was, she didn't trust herself. Not when it came to Ethan. She fled before she lost what small sense she still possessed. Vaguely, she was aware of someone strolling over to talk with Ethan at the booth.

But she was halfway across the diner on a return trip with a damp cloth and a coffee cup before the identity of the man registered.

She came to an immediate and abrupt halt. Coffee dribbled over the side of the mug. She made a move to do an about-face, but Ethan waved her over. And then for pride's sake, she became obligated to join them.

Ignoring her father, Dwight Fleming, she set down the coffee. But she felt her face flame.

Smiling, Ethan brought the cup to his lips. "Two of my favorite people in the whole world together in one place."

Her father pushed his glasses higher onto the bridge of his nose. "A sentiment I have a feeling Amber wouldn't share."

She scowled at her dad. "And I wouldn't be the only one, would I?"

A mother herded a trio of preschoolers through the narrow aisle toward a vacant table. Forcing Amber to lean closer to Ethan and out of their path. But diving for the counter stools, the three boys spun around like a pair of whirling tops.

"Reminds me of a certain young son of mine." Her dad threw Ethan a grin. "And his sidekick." Her father sobered. "Amber, I heard that with ErmaJean out of commission, Ethan is going to look after the girls until you graduate from nursing school. Is that true?"

"That's still up for debate." Heart pounding, she swiped the cloth over the table. "Not that it's any of your business."

Her father settled his hands on his hips. "It's Saturday. Who's keeping the girls today while you work?"

"Again, none of your business. But if you must know, Deirdre Fielding offered to let them spend the day at the dude ranch." Amber's lip curled. "You remember Mrs. Fielding, don't you, Dad? Mom's best friend."

Ethan set the mug onto the table with a clunk. "Amber."

"Yes, I remember Deirdre. A good woman, as was your mother." Her father's lips thinned. "I'm glad I ran into you, Amber. There's a serious matter I've been meaning to discuss with you about Lucy's and Stella's welfare."

She stilled. "What about Lucy and Stella?"

"It'll be summer soon. Have you thought about giving them swimming lessons?"

She folded her arms. "You can say that to me after what happened to Mom?"

"The kayak overturning and your mother getting caught underneath was a freak accident. You grew up on the water. I would be happy to give the girls lessons once school is out. It doesn't have to be me. Perhaps Ethan could—"

"I'm not letting the girls anywhere near the water." She jutted her jaw. "Or you either, Dad."

His expression hardening, her father's eyes flicked to Ethan. "Be careful with the girls." He grimaced. "Children will break your heart. Right, Amber?"

Feeling a sting of tears, Amber straightened so quickly she saw stars. "Why do you come into the Jar every week, Dad? It sure isn't for the food." She threw the cloth on the table. "To harass me or to gloat? Which is it?"

Ethan extricated himself from the booth. "Amber…" He reached for her.

She shook him off. "I'll get your lunch and leave you to your reunion with my father."

Trust her father to ruin the few moments of happiness she might've enjoyed with Ethan. Glaring at them both, she stalked away.

Chapter Five

The Mason Jar's kitchen door, with its glass porthole, swung shut behind Amber.

Sitting back down in the booth, Ethan found Dwight Fleming watching him watch his daughter. Behind Dwight's wire-rimmed glasses, there was an interesting gleam in his eyes Ethan wasn't sure how to interpret.

"I hate to see this bitterness between you and Amber. You two were always so close, Dwight."

There was no man Ethan respected more than Amber's father. He'd taught Ethan how to shave. How to read the river. How to be a man.

Brow furrowing, Dwight joined him on the other side of the booth. "Things change."

For a man in his late fifties, the rafting business had ensured Amber's father retained the shape of a man fifteen years younger. Dwight had the classic chiseled features of a man who'd spent his life outdoors. A former collegiate champion swimmer, his shoulders were still broad and powerful.

Ethan warmed his hands around the mug of coffee. "I was so sorry to hear about Mrs. Fleming's death."

For a second so brief as to be almost imaginary,

Dwight's stoic features wavered before resuming his customary mask of control. "Like the river, life flows on."

Ethan didn't believe him. Dwight had adored his wife. But Ethan respected his right to keep his feelings—and grief—to himself.

Co-owner of Fleming River Adventures, Kitty had been a perfect mix of outdoorsy athleticism and motherly warmth. Her sense of adventure had been legendary. And five years ago, her death on the river a tragic accident.

"If I'd have been able to get leave—"

"We know you would've been here if you could." Dwight fiddled with a sugar packet. "Your grandmother called me yesterday. She said you'd come home."

Is that what Truelove was? His home? Ethan wasn't sure anymore.

"Your grandmother isn't the only one hoping you'll decide to stay in Truelove for good."

"I'm only here until Grandma Hicks is back to her old self." Ethan shifted in the booth, the old familiar need to be away overtaking him. "I've got a job waiting in Wilmington, and next year I've promised myself a trip to test my skill on the Burnt Ranch Gorge in California."

"Class Five rapids." Dwight blew out a breath. "Serious sieves and hydraulics on that run."

Ethan grinned. "That's the challenge of it. Pitting yourself against the elements. The rush. The thrill. The—"

"The stupidity of risking your life trying to tame the untamable." Amber placed the hamburger plate, loaded with fries, on the table. "You two so totally deserve each other."

Dwight set his jaw. "Once upon a time you would've understood the love of white water."

She removed the order book from the pocket of her

jeans. "Once upon a time, I thought you loved us more than the river."

Dwight's face darkened. "You don't think I blame myself? Every day I—"

She ripped a paper from the pad. "Your bill." She laid it on the table in front of Ethan. "And you are just like…"

Ethan stiffened. "Just like who?"

She walked away.

"We still need to talk about the girls, Amber," he called.

"I never meant for things to get this bad between us." Dwight stared after her. "When her mom died, we were both hurting. I poured myself into the business. Matt was overseas. And I pegged Tony as no good the first time I met him. I should've never hired him."

Ethan's stomach knotted.

"Stuff was said—on both sides—that couldn't be taken back." Dwight eased out of the booth. "Lucy and Stella will grow up without me ever knowing them," he whispered.

Ethan got to his feet. "I'd love to stop by the office. Hang out. Like the old days, sir."

"Come by whenever you can." Dwight clapped his hand on Ethan's shoulder. "And don't think I won't try to convince you to reconsider giving Truelove another chance. You've got people who care about you here." Dwight's gaze wandered toward the kitchen. "You ever get tired of roaming, you could make a life here. A good life."

Problem was, Truelove wasn't Ethan's idea of a good life.

He had finished the burger and was halfway through the fries when Amber finally slipped into the empty seat Dwight had vacated.

She steepled her hands on the table. "I don't want you or Miss ErmaJean to think I'm not grateful. I admire your decision to allow your grandmother to recuperate in her own home."

Dropping his gaze, he shoved the plate away. Her admiration was unwarranted. His motivations were not as loving and unselfish as she believed. But he had the distinct feeling that if he shared the full terms of his agreement with Grandma, Amber would refuse him outright.

She took a breath. "I can't ask you to take on the care of two very lively—"

"You're not asking. I'm offering." How could he convince her? "It's important that you finish school."

"Be that as it may, you'll have enough on your hands taking care of your grandmother. And I... I don't want anyone's pity." Her cheeks pinked. "You have no idea how humiliating it is to always be on the receiving end of charity."

Something tore in his heart. "Don't be too sure about that, Amber. I'm the kid whose parents found it easy to abandon him. Think of me helping you as payback."

Amber's gaze flickered. "What do you mean?"

His throat thickened. "Payback for all the times your folks made me feel a part of your family. Like I belonged."

Reaching across the table, she laid her hand over his. "You did belong. They loved you, Ethan. We—" She pressed her lips together.

Then inspiration struck. He leaned forward. "What if we were to make a mutually beneficial deal?"

She gave him a look. "You and your deals."

"What if we could do each other a favor?"

Her forehead creased. "I don't understand."

"In the beginning, Grandma is going to need more

care than I can provide. What if you helped her with bathing and dressing? In turn, I could watch the girls so you can finish school." He pushed the plate of fries closer to her. "Help yourself."

"A lot of what-ifs." She snagged one of the fries. "You're proposing an exchange of services?"

"Exactly. No charity involved."

She twirled the fry in the pool of ketchup on the plate. "It *would* be awkward for you to help her with such personal needs." She bit off the end of the fry.

He decided Amber even chewed pretty. "So what do you say? You'd be doing me a favor, Amber."

Swallowing, she studied him for a long moment. "I guess there's no harm in giving it a try."

Over the rest of the fries, they worked out a schedule.

Her accelerated nursing classes ran Tuesdays and Thursdays from five in the evening till ten o'clock at night. On those days, he would be responsible for the girls until Amber returned from class. He would also be on twin-duty every other weekend on the Saturdays and Sundays when she had clinicals. Every day after her shift, Amber would tend to his grandmother. Ethan would take over afternoon carpool.

Ethan glanced at his cell. "I'm due to pick up Grandma from the hospital in a few hours."

Amber ate the last fry. "I'll meet you at the house and get her settled." She slid out of the booth. "My lunch break is over."

"Fries aren't lunch, Amber."

She shrugged. "Got to get to work."

He didn't think she took proper care of herself, but he knew better than to say anything. She'd only tell him to mind his own business. So they parted. Amber went into the kitchen. And he left to buy a shower chair for his grandmother per Amber's suggestion.

Later, when he pulled into the driveway with his grandmother, Amber was waiting on the porch. Dusting off her jeans, she stood up.

He met her halfway. "I hope we didn't keep you waiting long. I had to go by the pharmacy to get Grandma's prescriptions."

"No problem. I finished my shift at three." She inspected her wristwatch. "There's still time before I have to pick up the girls from the Fieldings'."

He went around to retrieve the wheelchair from the trunk. Amber opened ErmaJean's door and hugged her.

"I can't thank you enough for helping Ethan with my care."

Amber shook her head. "I don't feel right about getting paid to do something I'd want to do, anyway."

Thinking over their arrangement, earlier he'd texted Amber about adding a financial compensation to their agreed-upon exchange of services.

"I was going to have to hire someone for Grandma's at-home care." He brought the chair over. "It would cost me a lot more to hire someone from an agency. I'd prefer the money go to you."

His grandmother patted Amber's hand. "I feel better having you here instead of a stranger."

Amber stepped aside as he maneuvered the chair closer to the car.

"It's a win for all of us, Amber." He set the chair brakes. "Swapping services to everyone's benefit."

She worried her lower lip with her teeth. "I want you both to know how much I appreciate this opportunity to finish school. And the extra money will enable me to reduce my hours at the Mason Jar. Giving me more time to study for finals."

He helped his grandmother stand, careful she didn't bear any weight on her fractured leg. Amber held on to his grandma, providing stability as he transitioned her into the wheelchair.

"Whew!" Grandma flopped into the chair. "That was a workout."

He released the brake. "The chair is only for trips away from home." Gripping the chair handles, he pushed his grandmother up the drive.

Amber strolled beside them. "I'll show you how to use the crutches."

Grandma groaned.

Amber squeezed her shoulder. "We'll go over everything together. I promise."

Past the clump of daffodils at the corner of the house, Ethan pushed the chair around to the ramp he'd erected.

Grandma put her hand to her throat. "Oh, Ethan, honey. How did you ever have time to build this?"

Flicking a look at Amber, he broadened his chest. "I'm a fast worker."

Amber rolled her eyes. As he'd meant her to. "You're something, all right."

"It was fun using Granddad's tools." He leveraged the wheelchair over the doorjamb into the kitchen. "Now you can enjoy being a lady of leisure, Grandma. The queen bee."

Grandma sniffed. "I've always been queen bee around here."

"Don't worry, Miss ErmaJean." Amber poked Ethan's biceps with her finger. "I'll make sure he doesn't forget it."

"I'm not likely to forget." He made a face. "Not with all you females around to remind me."

"Let's get Miss ErmaJean on the sofa."

With Amber's guidance, he transferred his grand-mother to the couch. She propped the older woman against the cushions. "For the first few days, we need to keep your leg elevated, level with your heart, to reduce any swelling."

Grandma smoothed her skirt. "We've been invited to a picnic at the Jackson orchard on Sunday, Ethan. Callie's father, Nash, and her husband, Jake, will help you feel not quite so outnumbered."

"But that's tomorrow." He placed a pillow under her casted leg. "Are you sure you'll feel up to it, Grandma?"

She fluttered her hand. "Miss a chance to see the apple trees in bloom? I think not. Besides, I'm already sick of being stuck indoors."

His gaze darted to Amber.

"Resuming normal activity with some limitations is a good thing," she assured him. "It's important to keep up a patient's spirits."

"Exactly." Grandma smiled. "Seeing as this is Amber's weekend off from clinicals, it will give you and the girls a chance to get used to each another before twin-sitting begins Monday afternoon."

"Which reminds me." Amber tucked a throw around his grandmother. "I need to go over the car pool diagram with Ethan."

He handed his grandmother the remote. "How hard can picking up a pair of munchkins from school be?"

The women exchanged amused looks.

Amber pursed her lips. "Let's just say there are certain protocols that must be followed." She turned to his grandmother. "Make sure to wiggle your toes often. It will reduce stiffness."

He shrugged. "I can do rules."

Amber propped her hand on her hip. "Since when?"

"Since joining the Marines." He smirked. "I can do adulting, Amber."

Grandma gave an unladylike snort. "Let's hope so."

"Relax, ladies. I got this." Hands tucked into his armpits, he rocked onto his heels. "Two little girls. School. Car. Throw open the door."

And because he knew it would irritate Amber, he flashed his trademark Ethan Green smile. "I might even decide to slow down before they jump in."

Grandma's eyes widened. "Ethan!"

Tongue pressed into her cheek, Amber shook her head. "He's just trying to push my buttons, Miss ErmaJean."

He raised his eyebrow. "Is it working?"

A small smile played about Amber's lips. "I learned a long time ago never to take you too seriously."

He straightened. "All kidding aside, I want you to know I take your children's safety and well-being very seriously, Amber." But then he couldn't help adding, "You saw what I did there? Children? 'Kidding'?"

She laughed. He loved to make her laugh. The lighthearted banter was their way with each other. Always had been. And though his time in Truelove might be temporary, he decided to make it his personal mission to help Amber laugh more often.

"It'll be fine. They'll be fine," he said to reassure himself as much as Amber. "What could go wrong?"

Ethan woke Sunday morning with a strange sense of trepidation. He hadn't been inside a church since he'd lived in Truelove. And he wasn't sure how he felt about returning to the little chapel where his grandmother had taken him—most times against his will—every Sunday of his childhood.

He hadn't minded the Bible stories or the songs. But it had been hard to sit still when he longed to be outside in the sunshine. He was a grown-up now, supposedly anyhow. Yet he remained much more comfortable with doing rather than merely being.

Grandma never missed a service, and he didn't have the heart to disappoint her. After a quick text from his grandmother, IdaLee stopped by to help her dress.

Afterward, he loaded Grandma into the sedan and headed to the white clapboard church. Nestled in a glade on the edge of town, the steeple brushed a picture-perfect Blue Ridge sky.

He wheeled his grandmother from the gravel parking lot over the tiny footbridge, spanning the small creek. Rushing water burbled over the moss-covered stones. Above the soft murmur of voices were sweet sounds of birdsong. The apple-green leaves of a willow rustled in a light breeze.

Utilizing the handicapped ramp, he rolled his grandmother into the sanctuary and parked her at the end of a pew. "The prodigal grandson returns," he murmured.

"Your words, dear heart." She touched his hand. "Never mine."

A sudden lump in his throat, he hung back as her many friends engulfed her in hugs.

"Miss ErmaJean is a favorite here in Truelove."

His pulse leaped at the sound of Amber's voice.

In a figure-flattering yellow sundress, she looked as fresh as springtime. And she smelled delicious. Like lilacs.

"Where are the girls?" he asked, his voice gruff.

"I've taken them to children's church. Trust me." Her lips twitched. "It's better for everyone's contemplation, if they're age-appropriately occupied."

"Makes me wish there'd been children's church when I was a kid."

Amber batted her lashes. "You made the elders wish it, too. Much to the benefit of subsequent generations."

"So you're saying I'm highly influential?" He stuck his tongue in his cheek. "A trendsetter. A legacy builder."

"Don't oversell it, Ethan." She jabbed her finger into his chest. "You are impossible."

He grinned. "That's why you love me."

She blinked, a startled look in her eyes. "Y-you wish." Brushing past him, she slipped across the aisle into a pew with Callie and a dark blond man Ethan presumed to be her husband, Jake McAbee.

When the prelude music started, he edged around his grandmother's chair and sat in the pew. Huge, hand-hewn beams soared above his head. Stained glass windows depicted Bible stories. Finding his childhood favorite, he was surprised at the rush of happy memories, of the faith his grandmother had sought to instill within him.

A community of faith. He was glad Amber would be able to give Lucy and Stella this—roots. Something he had never wanted. Until now?

During the opening song, he held the green-bound hymnal for his grandmother. And tried not to stare at Amber's blond hair brushing against her shoulder blades. At the last minute, a muscular yet lanky guy scooted into the pew beside her.

Reverend Bryant called the congregation to prayer. Ethan was struck by how the man talked to God like He was right there beside him. Like talking to a friend. As natural as breathing.

Another sweet memory rose—of Ethan's grandparents' prayers over him as a boy. Without a doubt, it had been his grandmother's prayers that kept him alive in Afghanistan. And God's grace.

For the first time in a long while, he bent his head, giving thanks to God for preserving him. For allowing him to return to Truelove. For enabling him to return—home?

Then Reverend Bryant gripped the sides of the pulpit. "Pride, my dear brothers and sisters, is what keeps us from experiencing God's favor in our lives."

Funny, he'd just been thinking about God's grace. God's favor. Same thing.

He leaned back against the pew. Had a misplaced pride caused him to view Truelove through the lens of his father's desertion? Had he truly been as outcast as he'd felt?

Bending forward, he rested his elbows on his thighs and laced his hands together. Pride—another name for his determination to keep everyone at arm's length. Other than Matt and Grandma, allowing no one to get close enough to hurt him again.

His former girlfriend, Kelly, had accused him of being emotionally distant. He was vaguely aware he ought to be more torn up about losing her. But perhaps her rejection had stung his self-confidence more than his heart. As to his inability for intimacy, Kelly might've been onto something.

A further startling realization dawned. How long had it been since he called his mother? Sure, she'd remarried and moved away. But feeling replaced by her new husband—and prideful—it was Ethan who'd chosen not to go with her into her new life.

God hates pride, the reverend warned.

What would his life look like if Ethan stopped keeping everyone—including God—at arm's length? What if he could trust God not to hurt him? What if he opened his life to Him?

At the closing hymn, Ethan rose with the congregation. He resolved to ponder the ramifications of what his pride had cost him. Later, when he could sort through the confusing tangle of emotions he was only now beginning to confront, to understand.

By the time the other half of the congregation had jumped up to love on his grandmother, Amber and Callie had disappeared through the door flanking the pulpit. Probably to get their kids.

Almost the last to leave the church, he steered the car toward the Jackson family orchard. Pink redbuds and white dogwoods dotted the slopes of the tree-studded Blue Ridge. Descending into the valley, he emerged into slightly gentler terrain. Horses grazed in pastures. A couple of miles later, he pulled off the main highway and drove under the crossbars. Bypassing a rustic country store, he continued on the long gravel-covered drive.

Grandma smiled. "It's so beautiful this time of year at Apple Valley Farm."

The leafed-out apple trees were at their peak, and a shower of petal pink blossoms carpeted the road. Set on a knoll overlooking the orchard, the tin roof of the two-story white farmhouse gleamed in the afternoon sun.

A bevy of vehicles occupied the yard. One of them, a navy blue pickup, had a for-sale sign stuck in the rear windshield. "Looks like they've invited the whole town." He helped his grandmother transfer to the wheelchair.

"Just a few close friends and neighbors."

A long table with chairs had been placed under the shade of a flowering cherry tree. The screened door creaked open and slapped shut as Callie scurried out with a large bowl of potato salad.

"Dad and Jake are at the grill cooking the chickens." She gestured toward the flume of smoke rising from a black-barreled, monster cooker near the barn. "Pour yourself some tea. We'll eat as soon as Lorena arrives from the hospital." Depositing the plastic-wrapped bowl on the table, Callie headed for the house.

Ethan fixed his grandmother a glass of sweet tea. "Remind me who Lorena is."

"Lives next door. Good friend to Callie's late mother." Grandma took a sip and sighed. "Now, that hits the spot. What was I saying? Oh, yes, Lorena is also an emergency room nurse. She helped Amber get into the accelerated program."

He heard the sound of children's voices first. Then he spotted Lucy, Stella and a slightly younger boy racing between the rows of apple trees.

"Who does the little boy belong to, Grandma?"

"He's Jonas Stone's little boy. Jonas was several years ahead of you in high school. You may not have crossed paths. His family owns the dude ranch."

Ethan shook his head. "I'm not sure—"

"That's him." His grandmother pointed.

A tall man in a brown cowboy hat ambled out of the orchard with Amber. The same man who'd sat beside her in church.

Ethan scowled. "Shouldn't he be with his wife?"

"Hush now," Grandma hissed. "He'll hear you. Jonas lost his wife. He and Amber have that in common. He's a good man."

Good enough for Amber? Ethan snorted, taking an instant and completely unjustified dislike to Stone.

Seeing them, Amber waved and came over. She kissed his grandmother's cheek and straightened. "Hey, Ethan."

He grunted.

Amber tilted her head. "What's wrong with you?"

"Nothing." He stuck his hand out to Stone. "Don't believe we've met."

"Oh, that's right." Amber's eyes flitted from Ethan to Stone. "Ethan Green, meet my friend Jonas Stone."

Friend, huh? What was with women and cowboys?

He shook Stone's hand. "It's *old* friends who make the best friends."

Stone winced.

Ethan left off making mincemeat of Stone's hand to find his grandmother studying him over the rim of her tea glass, amusement dancing in her eyes.

A woman in purple scrubs exited the SUV that had driven into the yard.

Grandma nudged his arm. "I have it on good authority, we're in for an announcement this afternoon." She licked her lips. "Another successful match in Truelove, where true love awaits."

An announcement? What kind of— His gaze swung from Amber to Jonas Stone. Something went cold in his belly.

"Efan! Efan! Efan!" Lucy shrieked.

Running full bore, she captured Ethan around the knees, nearly knocking him off his feet. Stella's approach was more sedate, less eager. More like a funeral march. Stone moved to intercept his small son from a collision course with a flower bed.

Lucy lifted her arms to him. Ethan glanced at Amber.

She shrugged. "Lucy, you're too big to be carried around like a baby. But go ahead. Hold her if you want to, Ethan."

When he did, Lucy draped her arms around his neck and gave him a big hug. "I missed you, Efan."

His heart puddled a little. "It's good to know somebody's glad to see me, Lucy Lou." He poked her belly with his finger. Writhing, she giggled.

Amber's brow knitted. "What's that supposed to mean?"

People said women had mood swings. So what was up with Ethan?

But apparently, he'd already won over one of Amber's daughters. Another member of the Ethan Green fan club. Like mother, like daughter?

"Mommy?" Stella tugged at Amber's skirt. "Maisie said after lunch we could ride the tractor with her dad."

Absentmindedly, she brushed her hand over Stella's head. "We'll see."

But things got too hectic for further reflection. She helped Callie, Lorena and Jonas's mom, Deirdre Fielding, carry the rest of the potluck items to the table. Then Amber's children had to be corralled and semicontained in adjacent chairs.

ErmaJean introduced Ethan to Jake and three-year-old Maisie. As usual, adoring Maisie was stuck to her father tighter than a deer tick. Coming around to fix Lucy's and Stella's plates, Amber patted the sweet little girl's blond bouncing curls.

Amber wondered if Ethan felt like an outsider. He had the same look on his face like years ago when he'd go quiet at the noisy, happy Fleming dinner table. A wistful hunger for something that had nothing to do with food.

Yesterday at the diner when he'd spoken of his deep-seated feelings of alienation, it was the first time he'd ever shared anything so personal with her. Mr. Too Cool for School had always laughed off his hurts. Hidden his pain. A tough guy who didn't usually reveal any vulnerability.

And today he was looking everywhere but at her. Maybe why he was acting so oddly. Embarrassed that he'd shown weakness. Such a guy attitude. Although not necessarily a condition confined to men. She struggled with her own pride issues.

But she felt honored that he'd trusted her. Giving her an insight into why he believed there was nothing for him in Truelove.

Everyone had wounds. She agonized over how badly she and Tony might've already damaged her girls. Daily she prayed God wouldn't allow her issues to stand between what He wanted to do in her children's lives.

"May I have your attention, please?" Rising, Nash tapped his butter knife against his glass. "Lorena, sweetheart?" He took her hand.

Even the children quieted. Somewhere, a robin sang.

"Dad, if you don't go ahead and tell it, I'm going to burst from excitement," Callie said.

Everyone laughed.

Nash smiled. "We've already told the family and received their blessing, but we wanted the rest of you to know, at long last, Lorena has consented to make me the happiest man on earth."

"It's about time," ErmaJean huffed.

Hugs and well-wishes ensued. The children clapped enthusiastically, sensing the joy.

ErmaJean touched Amber's arm. "This match took some doing, let me tell you, missy." She winked. "But GeorgeAnne, IdaLee and I proved equal to the task. We applied reverse psychology."

As Amber remembered it, they'd tried to match Callie's widowed father to every single lady of a certain age in the county. Everyone except Lorena. And tried setting up Lorena with every middle-aged bachelor. Except Nash Jackson.

"I love it when a plan comes together. With nowhere

else to run, they ran straight into each other's arms."
ErmaJean waggled her finger. "There's more than one
way to peel an apple."

The matchmakers had never attempted to pair Amber
with anyone. Probably writing her off as a lost cause.
After all, what man in his right mind would come within
a mile of a single mom with two little girls?

For the hundredth time, she tamped down the insidi-
ous fear that no man would ever be able to get past the
fact that she'd been married—albeit so disastrously—to
someone else.

Eager to distract herself from gloomy thoughts, she
started clearing away the empty plates.

"Absolutely not." Callie shooed her away. "Consider
yourself off duty today."

Callie had been a true friend. Sticking by Amber
through thick and thin. With Lucy and Stella getting
restless, Ethan suggested they take the girls to expend
some energy on Maisie's nearby swing set. Amber read-
ily agreed.

He deposited Lucy into one of the swings, but when he
reached for Stella, she shrank into Amber. She'd noticed
Stella avoided contact with him. Her daughter wasn't
afraid of him, though. Just wary.

Something Amber would do well to emulate. A
guarded heart was a safe heart.

Lucy's and Stella's feet dangled above the grass.

"Hang on, Lucy Lou." Standing behind her, he pulled
on the chains. "Are you ready, Stella Bella?"

Rosebud lips tight, Stella faced forward, not respond-
ing.

Amber pulled Stella's swing level with where Ethan
held Lucy. "I'm sorry." Another thing she admired about

him—one of many—his persistence in trying to connect with Stella.

"No worries. But you Fleming ladies need to remember that I don't quit." He quirked his eyebrow. "If anything, a challenge makes victory all the sweeter." He let go of the swing, and Lucy sailed through the air.

"Me, Mommy. Me." Stella bounced.

Ethan smiled at her, and Amber lost her hold on the chain. Stella swung forward, though not as far or fast.

"Higher," Lucy called. "Faster, Efan."

With a gentle prod, he sent her swooping again.

"I'm f-whying, Stehwaa!" she shouted. "I'm bigger than you."

Amber grimaced. "Uh-oh."

Stella bunched her muscles and pumped her legs, but try as she might she couldn't attain the same aerial height as her twin. "Mommy!" she implored. "I want to go like Lucy."

"Competitive little darlings, aren't they?" Ethan murmured.

With another push, she sent Stella airborne once more. "But despite their squabbling, woe to the outsider who dares to hurt their sister."

"I think it's sweet. I always wished I had a brother or sister."

The pensive tone had returned to his voice.

"Matt and I tried to make you feel like our honorary sibling."

"You were Matt's sister. Not mine." Ethan's hazel eyes sharpened. "Do you think of me as a brother?"

"N-no," she stammered.

He gave her a crooked smile. "Good." He sent Lucy winging.

"Mommy!" Stella protested. "Push harder."

Amber crossed her arms. "I'm not as strong as Ethan. If you want to go as high and fast as Lucy, Ethan is the only one who can get you to where you want to go."

She blushed. Far more truth in that than she cared to contemplate. Stella's swing slowed.

"Okay," Stella called at last. "Ethan, would you, please…?"

"Your wish is my command, Stella Bella." Taking Amber's place, he gave her a mighty shove. Squealing with glee, Stella soared high away from the ground.

Ethan's mood seemed to have improved. And because he'd been transparent enough to share a piece of his heart with Amber, she felt compelled to return the favor.

"You've never asked me about… About…" Amber moistened her lips.

He kept both girls zooming toward the treetops. "About what?"

"About Tony. My ex-husband." She spared a glance to make sure the twins were too occupied to overhear. "Their biological father."

He staggered, momentarily losing his footing. "I didn't want to pry."

She laughed, though not with mirth. "Well, that would make you the only one in Truelove."

He gave her the lopsided grin that buckled her knees. "Gotta love Small Town, USA." He immediately sobered. "But if it's too painful, you don't have to tell me anything."

"The whole thing was painful." She swallowed. "From beginning to end. But lately, I've felt better able to process it. Let it go."

An emotional healing she suspected she owed as much to Ethan's return to Truelove as anything else.

"Didn't Miss ErmaJean tell you what happened?"

"Only that *he* worked for your father at the rafting company."

The way Ethan said "he" made clear his opinion of the twins' father. She appreciated Ethan's unreserved loyalty. She'd known little of that since the fateful summer she met Tony. Loyalty and honesty were everything to her now.

"The last thing I heard about you from Matt was that you were at college."

She took a breath. "I'd finished my junior year when I came home that May to work the summer season with Mom and Dad. But Mom—" Her voice broke.

"Matt said your mother was trying to rescue a kid trapped on the river."

Amber nodded. "There'd been a lot of spring rain. The river was high and fast. From the outset, it was going to be dicey. I wanted to call for a swift water helo rescue, but Dad was afraid the boy wouldn't last that long. He wanted to go in alone, but you know Mom—" Her voice quavered. "You knew Mom. She wasn't one to let things happen without her."

"If Matt and I had been here…"

"The what-ifs are the quickest way to melancholy. You and Matt were serving our country." She injected a teasing note in her voice. "Saving the world from tyranny."

He gave her a small smile. "There is that."

"You know the rest of the story. Dad saved the boy. He couldn't save Mom. By the end of summer, he'd turned completely into himself. I was so unhappy and alone. Tony made me feel something besides numb."

Ethan dropped his gaze, continuing to send Stella and Lucy skyward.

"I quit college and went off with him." She looked away. "But I had hardly been married a month before I realized I'd made a mistake I figured I'd spend the rest of my life regretting."

"Was he cruel to you? Did he hurt you?" Ethan's voice sounded strangled.

Her gaze returned to his. "No. But I'd married Peter Pan, you see. A happy-go-lucky, never-wants-to-grow-up wanderer. In fairness, I think he soon realized he wasn't cut out for marriage. Of course by that time, I was pregnant and he freaked."

Ethan's eyes blazed, but she understood his anger wasn't directed at her. "A decent man doesn't walk away from his children, nor his wife."

He was thinking of his own father. Amber touched his shoulder. "No, he doesn't."

A muscle jumped in his cheek. "You're better off without him."

"I think so, too."

"His loss."

As if her hand possessed a life of its own, she brushed her fingertip along his jaw. "Your father, too."

Something raw blazed from his eyes before he clamped it down into the region Ethan stored his emotions. "Do the girls ever hear from him?"

"No. They don't even share his last name." She dropped her hand, appalled at her boldness. "Last I heard through the rafting grapevine, Tony is somewhere out West. On yet another freewheeling adventure."

Ethan's brows bunched. "Do the girls ask about him?"

Her eyes flitted toward Callie and Jake, chatting with ErmaJean. "Only since Maisie found her daddy last autumn."

"I didn't realize…"

"Callie and Jake have only been married since November. It's a long story. I'll tell you about it another time."

"I like the sound of that." He nodded. "It's a date."

She blinked, but he stepped away to help the girls. They'd grown tired and wished to disembark their chariots to the sky. Amber decided he probably hadn't meant that the way it sounded. As in a "date-date." Probably something more along the lines of a calendar "date."

Don't be a silly fool, she told herself. *Don't read more into what's there.*

They were friends, nothing more. Doing each other a favor. And though it appeared he'd dropped his plan to relocate Miss ErmaJean, she would be wise to remember he'd eventually return to the beach. This interlude with Ethan was too good to be true. Too good to last.

After the catastrophe with Tony, Amber didn't believe in happily-ever-afters.

Chapter Six

Monday had barely begun before Grandma Hicks started worrying about an upholstery job she owed a client. "I usually work in your granddad's shop, but if you tote the chair into the dining room along with my tools, I think I could finish the project."

Ethan nursed his second cup of coffee. "You're supposed to be resting, Grandma. And with your leg in a cast, your maneuverability is iffy. The customer will have to wait until you're better."

She got the stubborn glint in her eye he recognized all too well. "But I promised."

"Not happening, Grandma. For the time being, you've got to accept you have limitations."

"The chair is his wife's favorite. It's supposed to be her birthday gift." His grandmother wrung her hands. "I've never failed a customer before. People in the community know if your granddad or I promised something, our word was our bond."

"People in the community should also know sometimes life gets in the way of even the best-laid plans."

Her lips thinned with disapproval. "If you don't have your reputation, what else matters?"

She wasn't going to let this go.

Ethan blew out a breath. "When is the birthday?"

"Her husband was hoping to give it to her tonight."

"What?" He half rose.

"I hate to disappoint them." She looked at him and then away. "You're right, of course. It's probably too much for me to tackle in my condition."

He sat down again. "Glad you're seeing sense."

"But it wouldn't be too much for you, Ethan."

His gaze snapped to hers.

"I've already removed the old fabric. It will be a breeze to re-cover. Not one of those tricky projects, like the channel-back chair you helped your granddad upholster that time." Her eyes misted. "It would make me so happy to see you working with his tools. Almost as good as having him here again."

And before Ethan knew what hit him, he found himself doing just that—re-covering the small old-fashioned lady's armchair in a gold-woven brocade. He spent the entire morning in the shop.

He would've finished sooner, but he couldn't resist doing a bit of restoration to the carved wooden rosettes scrolled across the top of the chair. The client swung by after lunch to collect the chair and pay Ethan's grandmother. The guy was effusive in his praise.

Although Ethan's muscles ached from the unaccustomed bending, he felt good about a job well-done. And he experienced a satisfaction he hadn't expected from using the tools of his late grandfather's trade.

Later that afternoon, inching forward in the car pool lane, Ethan reckoned he'd been less nervous storming terrorist strongholds in Fallujah. Having temporarily forsaken the Harley, he felt conspicuously unmanly in his grandmother's cute lime-green sedan. Cute only if you were a grandma. Or a girl.

But things could be worse. He frowned at the two vehicles boxing him in line. He could be driving a minivan.

The playground was empty. An American flag waved proudly on a pole outside the school entrance. Not yet old enough for kindergarten, the girls were enrolled in an extended-day, head start program for economically disadvantaged children.

It killed him to think about how hard Amber worked. The sacrifices she unflinchingly made. He wasn't sure he'd ever loved anyone—save Grandma—like that.

The dismissal bell rang promptly at three o'clock. His stomach knotted. He peered through the hordes of children rapidly exiting the brick building. A cluster of children huddled under the open breezeway on the sidewalk.

He spotted the twins almost immediately. Tiny compared to the older kids. Stella, typically solemn. Lucy, who'd never met a stranger. And if for no other reason than they reminded him of Amber, already they tugged at his heart.

They were so stinking cute. Their blond hair had for the most part teased loose from the braids Amber so carefully fashioned this morning.

Catching sight of him at the wheel, Lucy's face lit up. His heart did a strange lurch. In his lifetime, there hadn't been many people excited to see him.

Grandma had been one. The old Amber possibly being the other. And now her adorable daughters. At least, one of them. Lucy waved wildly at him. Stella glared fixedly at the pavement.

A school staff member opened the back door. Lucy scooted over the seat and into her booster. Stella reluctantly clambered inside.

The car pool monitor shut the door, and he pulled away from the curb and out toward the street. "So, ladies… Did you make it a good one?"

Lucy chattered away. She recounted in enthusiastic detail about writing her numbers on the whiteboard. And about some upcoming community fund-raiser dance. He recalled seeing the signs posted around town.

Rounding the square, he headed down Main. During Lucy's monologue, he nodded and grunted in the appropriate places.

The Sweetheart Dinner/Dance was going to be held in the square. Lucy wanted to go so, so badly. It would be fun. She would pretend to be a princess. Everyone in their class was going. Townspeople, too. She ticked off the names of everyone of her acquaintance. It was a long list.

When she finally wound down, Ethan quickly interjected. "Your mom tells me you love art, Stella. What did you make at school today?"

His gaze flicked to the rearview mirror. A scowl marred Stella's perfect brow. She said nothing, just stared out the window at the passing scenery.

He set his jaw. He was going to win over Stella Fleming if it killed him. Which, at this rate, it might.

Leaving the outskirts of town, Stella lifted her eyes when they passed the sign that said Welcome to Truelove. "This isn't the way to Gigi's."

"I thought we'd take a quick detour. Meet some friends of mine I think you'd enjoy."

"Yay!" Lucy cheered.

Stella pointed an accusing finger. "After school, you're supposed to take us to Gigi's." Like her mother, Stella had trust issues.

Her twin pouted. "It's a field twip, Stehwaa."

Stella shook her head. "Gigi is waiting for us."

He smiled into the mirror. "Gigi packed snacks for us to share with my friends."

"Snacks?" Lucy leaned forward, stretching the belt harness. "For us, too? Awe dey yummy?" In signature Lucy fashion, she didn't wait for him to respond. "Awen't you hungwy, Stehwaa? I'm hungwy, Efan."

"Gigi made sure there are enough yummy snacks for all of us."

Stella—so much like her mom—wasn't as easily won over. "We have homework." She narrowed her eyes at him. "Mommy says we must always do our homework."

"And we will." He steered the car past Apple Valley Farm. How much homework could a four-year-old have? "Soon as we visit my friends."

"Dat's Maisie's house." Lucy motioned as they by-passed the orchard.

"When I was your age, your mommy, Maisie's mommy—Callie, Uncle Matt and I were the best of friends."

"Maisie used to be wike us, but she has a daddy now." Lucy gave him a look out of the corner of her lashes. "Do *you* fink someday we will get a daddy?"

Two thoughts occurred to Ethan so quickly as to be nearly simultaneous. One—Lucy was going to be a hand-ful in about ten years. *Dear God, help the mountain boys.*

And two—some guy becoming their father and Am-ber's husband rubbed Ethan the wrong way.

"Efan?"

He opened his mouth, but Stella beat him to the punch.

"No, Lucy," Stella scolded. "Maisie's daddy got lost, but then he found her. He always loved her."

Lucy jutted her jaw. "Our daddy got wost. When our new daddy finds us, he'll always wuv us, too."

Stella snorted. "Daddies don't work that way, Lucy."

"They do." Lucy's voice rose. "You fink you know ev-wee-fing but you don't. Not about daddies."

Stella pushed Lucy's shoulder. "I do so know."

Lucy shoved back. "You don't."

"Girls!" He cut in as the wrangling escalated.

He frowned at them in the mirror. He'd negotiated peace settlements between rival warlords less fractious than these two. Weren't girls supposed to be easier to handle?

Venturing beyond the turnoff to the trailer, he drove onto a farm road. "Hang on to your hats." He gripped the wheel as the sedan jostled along the pitted track.

Lucy giggled. "We awen't wear-wing hats, siwee Efan."

Stella's mouth resumed its normal pinched appearance. Her default expression with him. Rounding the curve of the winding road, the car emerged on the other side of the glade of trees.

Ethan braked beside the small pond, sending up a swirl of dust. "We're here."

He waited for the dust to settle before getting out. Opening the rear door, he leaned inside to help Lucy unfasten the booster buckle. She scrambled down.

Ethan reached to help Stella but, pressing the lever, she released the safety harness by herself. With a little sniff of pride, she scooted out and brushed past him to where Lucy waited.

"Where are your fwiends, Efan?"

He retrieved the bag with their snacks and closed the door.

Gasping, Stella gestured at the pond. "Look!" A flotilla of brown and white ducks floated into view.

Score one in his ongoing quest to connect with the notoriously hard-to-impress Stella. Who, like her mother, appeared impervious to his widely acknowledged charms.

"Baby ducks!" Lucy shrieked, dancing in the grass.

"Shh..." He put his fingers to his lips. "Not so loud. You'll scare the ducklings away."

Eyes big as dinner plates, both girls froze, Lucy in midclap. Only the busy drone of bumblebees in a nearby patch of clover broke the near-DEFCON silence that suddenly reigned. He was going to have to remember that. He needed every trick he could muster in his twin-sitting toolkit.

"How would you girls like to give my friends an afternoon snack?" he whispered.

"Yummy snacks," Lucy reminded him in a softer indoor voice.

He lifted a sandwich bag in each hand.

Stella scowled at the kernels of sweet corn. "Not yummy."

He'd done his research. Bread wasn't a healthy choice for ducks. "Corn is yummy to ducks."

And frozen peas. Oats. Rice, too.

He winked at them. "After we feed them, Gigi sent other kinds of snacks yummy to little girls' tummies, I promise."

Both girls reached for the bags.

He held on a moment more. "Remember, we have to go slowly. No sudden movements or noise. No arguing. We don't want to frighten them."

Lucy gazed earnestly at him. "We won't be bad, Efan. We pwomise, don't we, Stehwaa?"

Had someone told them they were bad? It wouldn't have been Amber or his grandmother, who believed the sun rose and set with these small pip-squeaks.

Then a memory from his own boyhood hollowed his

gut. Maybe no one had needed to tell them. Perhaps the lack of a father had already convinced them there was something inherently bad about them.

As if somehow he wasn't—they weren't—as good or worthy as other children. In a child's mind, when your own parents leave you, there must be something wrong with you.

Only with maturity and Dwight Fleming's interaction in his life had Ethan come to realize the fault lay not so much within himself as with the two very flawed human beings who'd given him life.

He crouched. "Lucy, you and Stella aren't bad."

Brows bunched, Lucy tilted her head. "Miss G'Anne says we act too wild."

He locked gazes with her. "You are not too wild. And even if sometimes you forget and are noisy, you two are good girls."

Stella slitted her eyes at him. "Even when we fight?"

"No one is perfect all the time. Even when you argue, you are still good, sweet girls."

High-spirited. Impulsive. Loud. But melted-butter wonderful in his humble but accurate opinion.

Lucy smiled. Stella's usual glower abated somewhat. Which, considering Stella, was a huge win for him. He'd take a win any way he could get one.

Clutching the bags, the twins crept forward on tiptoe. Perhaps overdoing his warning to be cautious. Resembling not so much a pair of children as pint-size cat burglars. He smiled. These girls cracked him up.

Lucy vibrated with barely contained glee. Stella, as was her way, was more self-contained in her joy. Only allowing herself a taste for fear it wouldn't, couldn't, last.

So much like her mother it made his heart ache. Making him more determined to paint a smile on Stella's stubborn, distrusting little face.

Once the first handful of corn was tossed into the water, the quacking ducks crowded the bank. The more aggressive ones waddled into the grass.

Lucy gave an excited squeal before clamping her free hand over her mouth. Wings flapping with eager greediness, a larger duck brushed against Stella's white tights. Instinctively, she drew back, plastering herself against Ethan for safety.

Kneeling beside the startled child, he placed one arm around Stella and with his other hand shooed the too-inquisitive creature. "It's okay, Stella. I'm here."

Biting her bottom lip, she frowned, but she didn't pull away.

"Let me show you girls something." Placing a handful of kernels in his palm, he held out his hand to a small duckling.

The brown-feathered baby bobbed forward, poking his yellow bill into Ethan's hand. Stella went rigid. Lucy sucked in a breath.

"It's okay," he said in a quiet voice. "I just keep my hand flat and my fingers out of the way."

The duckling quickly gobbled the remaining kernels.

"Let me t-why, Efan..." Lucy bobbed on her tiptoes. "Me next."

"No, Lucy." Stella took firm possession of his hand. "My turn first."

Swallowing a smile, he opened her hand and sprinkled a few kernels of corn on her palm. The duckling returned. Ethan laid his hand under hers as a support. When the duckling's bill touched her skin, Stella quivered.

He shot a quick glance at her, ready to snatch her hand

away, but a tiny smile hovered on the edge of her lips. A mixture of caution and dawning delight.

Not a bad way to approach new experiences and life in general.

Then Stella traded places with Lucy. They spent the next hour feeding the ducks. Running along the banks of the country pond. Exploring. Listening to birdcalls. Searching for four-leaf clovers. Munching on carrot sticks and celery.

After being cooped up indoors, they needed to run and play and be children. He felt an unusual affinity with them. A connection he'd not expected. He'd never spent much time—any time—with kids.

He wished someone had figured out his own rambunctious, younger self needed an appropriate outlet after school. Before attempting to settle down to homework. But he didn't blame his mother or grandparents. They'd been trying to make a living, keeping the business afloat.

Yet he might have had a better attitude toward school. Too often he'd turned his attention to more mischievous exploits. Hence, his troublemaker reputation.

Hands on his hips, he watched the girls toss handfuls of corn ever higher over the water to the ducks. Feeling pretty pleased with his ingenuity, he wondered why people believed it hard to take care of children.

This was easy. So simple. He was still congratulating himself right until the moment one of them fell into the shallow water at the edge of the pond.

Lucy, of course.

Webbed feet rapidly backpedaling, the ducks scattered to the hinterlands. And not to be outdone—or maybe she refused to let her twin have all the fun—Stella threw her fully clothed little self into the pond, too.

"Girls!" he shouted. But it was too late. He raced toward them.

Both stood up. Water ran in rivulets down their faces. Their dresses and once-pristine white tights were discolored with mud.

"Lucy! Stella! What have you done?"

They grinned at him.

"I'm a baby duck, Efan." Lucy splashed her sister.

"Stop splashing me, Lucy," Stella yelled.

Grimacing at the coldness of the water through his jeans, he waded into the pond to separate them.

Amber was going to kill him. Absolutely annihilate him.

Incredulous at the twins' bedraggled spectacle, he rested his hand on top of his head. Forget Amber— his grandmother would kill him before Amber had the chance.

Yeah, twin-sitting. Such a piece of cake. Not.

Amber laughed herself silly when she arrived to pick up the girls that evening, and ErmaJean told her of the girls' latest escapades.

"I don't know who was the most muddy…" ErmaJean smirked. "The kids or Ethan."

His hair still wet from the shower, Ethan gave her a sheepish smile. "Twin-sitting is harder than it looks."

"You don't say…" Amber smirked.

ErmaJean laughed. "Lucy and Stella aren't the only ones getting an education."

She escorted Ethan's grandmother to her bath while he helped Lucy and Stella finish their homework, which consisted mostly of practicing their letters on a child's handwriting tablet.

Afterward, Amber followed ErmaJean down the hall. "You're getting good on those crutches."

The older lady stopped on the threshold of the living room. "He's very good with them, isn't he?" She directed Amber's attention to where Ethan sat on the couch between Lucy and Stella. Although, characteristically, Stella had positioned herself at the far end of the sofa.

Amber never would've imagined Mr. Life of the Party could be so kind, gentle and thoughtful with her children. Or, for that matter, any children. But he was. More than she'd ever dreamed possible. With her, too.

"Dis was your favowite book when you was a boy, Efan?"

"Sure was." He opened the book. "I can't believe Grandma saved it all these years."

"What's it cawed, Efan?"

ErmaJean held her finger to her lips, but Amber needed no prompting.

"It's called *Make Way for Ducklings*." He underscored each word with his finger.

Lucy snuggled under his arm. "What's it about?"

"Mr. and Mrs. Mallard."

Lucy's face upturned. "And her children?"

Stella inched closer. "Baby ducks aren't children, Lucy. They're ducklings."

A smile tugging at his handsome lips, he flipped the page. "Right you are, Stella Bella. Anyone want to count the ducklings?"

"I do!"

Stella wriggled her way underneath his other arm. "I will."

"Looks like I've got my hands full." His gaze floated

between the girls. "Which means you two will have to help me turn the pages."

"Me!" Lucy raised her hand as if she were in the classroom.

Amber and ErmaJean exchanged amused looks, but Stella frowned.

"Maybe Stella Bella could put her finger under each word as I read the story. It's a big job." He scratched his neck. "Do you think you could handle that?"

She nodded vigorously, her braids bouncing. Then she bit her lip. "I may not know all the words, though."

He dropped his chin, his eyes boring into hers. "It's okay to not know everything. I'll help you."

Amber wasn't sure how he knew that, of the two, Stella was already reading, but somehow he did.

Neither Amber nor ErmaJean moved a muscle as he read the timeless classic to the girls. Both Lucy and Stella remained curled next to him, enraptured until the final word.

Tears blurred her eyes. He was so wonderful with the girls. Was there anything sweeter than a man cuddling his children and reading them a bedtime story?

Wait. They weren't his children. And Amber was shocked at how strongly she wished it were true.

She was also cut to the quick at the girls' obvious attachment to him—Stella, in spite of herself. ErmaJean had been right. Lucy and Stella needed a father figure.

If only a temporary one, she reminded herself. Ethan, like Tony, wasn't the sort of guy she could count on to stick around.

Miss ErmaJean shifted. Shaken out of her reverie, Amber caught her arm. "Are you all right?"

"I stood too long in one place, but I wouldn't have missed that for the world." ErmaJean's blue eyes crinkled at the corners. "A real treat, that's what it was. But I think I'll retire to my bedroom and finish the book Ida-Lee brought me today. Please let the girls say goodbye before y'all head out."

Amber stayed within arm's length of Ethan's grand-mother until she was safely ensconced in her favorite wingback chair. Returning, she found the living room deserted, except for Ethan.

Her heart thudded.

Ethan laid the picture book on the coffee table. "I think Stella's starting to thaw."

She scanned the room as if the girls might be hiding somewhere, but mainly to give herself time to get her pulse under control. "Where're Lucy and Stella?"

"I sent them into the kitchen to pack their backpacks." He patted the seat cushion. "How was your day?"

Her hesitation lasted about a millisecond before she sank onto the sofa. Who was she kidding? When it came to Ethan, she'd never been able to deny herself.

"Did you know there's an advertisement for Ethan Green Furniture Restoration tacked on the bulletin board at the Mason Jar?"

He rolled his eyes. "No, but I could guess who put it there."

She smiled. "Your grandmother isn't allowed to drive yet."

"But she's fully capable of making a phone call—excuse me—of texting her compatriots into doing her dirty work for her."

"The notice was written with an old-fashioned, ex-quisite penmanship."

He sighed. "IdaLee."

"I'd offer to take it down, but I value my life."

"My ears and the Truelove grapevine must've really

been burning this afternoon." He chuckled. "When I got back from the pond with the girls, there were five new projects waiting for me in Granddad's old shop. And Grandma claimed a sob story for each one."

Relaxing against the cushion, Amber smiled. "Do you mind?"

"I ought to…" He shook his head. "But somehow I don't. Might as well keep busy while I'm here. My mornings are free. Especially after GeorgeAnne called to tell me she'd be taking over Grandma's PT appointments."

"Best to keep busy," Amber agreed, her tongue firmly in her cheek. "Idle hands and all that. You don't want to lose your restoration skills."

"No danger of that." He smirked. "But if I do, I have lots of other skills."

She made sure he saw her roll her eyes. "You don't say."

He cocked his head. "Seeing is believing, baby cakes."

"You are some kind of *unbelievable*, Ethan Todd Green."

"Why, thank you, Amber Dawn Fleming." His eyes danced. "I agree. I'm unbelievably handsome, intelligent, debonair…"

She sniffed.

"Witty, charming, articulate—"

"Legend in your own mind."

They smiled at each other.

He stroked his beard-stubbled chin. "I can't imagine how I've managed without you all these years to keep me in my place."

"Stay and you won't have to imagine." Her cheeks went hot. She'd actually said that out loud?

His eyebrow arched. "Maybe I will. I might surprise you."

Ethan was full of surprises. But the biggest surprise of all was how he made her feel inside. An emotion she'd lost sight of until now.

Hope.

Chapter Seven

A couple weeks later in his granddad's shop, Ethan looked with satisfaction at the changes he'd wrought to the damaged drop leaf dining table. It had been a big job. He'd painstakingly sanded away the old finish.

He needed only to apply an oil-based varnish to allow the luster of the wood grain to shine through. He was reaching for the stain cloth when his cell phone buzzed on the workbench.

Intent on finishing the job, he nearly let it roll to voice mail, but he remembered his grandmother hadn't yet returned from her appointment. Miss GeorgeAnne had taken her to a follow-up visit with the orthopedist. So after quickly wiping his hands on the denim apron protecting his clothes, he grabbed the phone.

Glancing at the screen, sudden fear sliced through his gut. It was the school. "Hello?" His voice boomed louder than he intended.

"Mr. Green?" It was a woman on the other end. "Is this Ethan Green?"

His pulse thrummed. "Yes, this is Ethan Green."

"This is Principal Stallings. I've been unable to reach Lucy and Stella's mother or ErmaJean Hicks," the coolly impersonal voice informed him. "Your name and number were recently added to their contact information."

Amber had updated the forms when he took over afternoon car pool. If the school was calling, something had happened to the girls.

His heart jerked in his chest. "Are Lucy or Stella ill?"

"No." Principal Stallings paused. "But there's been an incident. You will need to come to the school office immediately."

A playground accident? Or worse? Sick fear knifed his gut. The fear of every parent on the planet.

Images exploded across his brain of one or both of the girls hurt. A hundred images raced through his mind of children on the evening news running from their schools amid gunfire.

"Principal Stallings..." His mouth went dry. "What's happened? Has there been a shooting?"

The woman inhaled sharply. "No, Mr. Green. But Lucy and Stella are in trouble. They've been involved in a fight with another student."

He stared at the phone in his hand. In a fight. Sweet Lucy? Quiet Stella?

"Principal Stallings, with all due respect, I can't believe—"

"It was not without provocation, but we have a zero tolerance policy toward violence at this school."

Lucy and Stella must be so scared. What had the other child done that would have incited the girls to do such a thing?

"I've spoken at length to each child. All three will receive the same disciplinary consequence."

"Which is?" he rasped.

"Considering this is their first offense, and they are only four years old, I've decided to send the girls home for the rest of the day. An unofficial suspension, but I would've been well within my rights to institute a much longer disciplinary action."

He raked his hand over his head. This would devastate Amber.

"I don't wish to derail their future academic career, so I've decided not to put the incident on their permanent records."

He glanced at the clock on the wall. Noon. Amber must be swamped with the lunch crowd. Maybe why she hadn't checked her phone. "Thank you, Principal Stallings. I appreciate your leniency."

"The other child's mother is on her way to school. I trust you can also shortly arrive?"

He was already walking out of the workshop. "I'll be there in five minutes."

"Their mother seems to have entrusted you, Mr. Green, with some responsibility for the twins' welfare. Though I'm not quite sure of your place in their lives."

Gravel crunched beneath his work boots. He wasn't quite sure of his place in Lucy's and Stella's lives, either. A temporary place. He was beginning to think God had put him in Truelove not only for his grandmother, but also for Amber and her children. Cradling the phone between his shoulder and his ear, he threw himself into the sedan and started the engine.

"Mr. Green, it is my sincere hope that you and the children's mother will stress to the twins the seriousness of what has happened today, and that this will never happen again."

Reiterating his promise to come quickly, he clicked off his phone and steered the car toward downtown Truelove. He drove around the square, bypassing the bustling café and hardware store. Veering into the school parking lot, he angled into a visitor space.

Despite what Principal Stallings had said, he couldn't in his wildest dreams imagine Lucy and Stella becoming involved in a schoolyard brawl. And he wouldn't allow them to be railroaded. He felt sure there was more to the story. It made his blood boil, thinking of some big lunkhead kid bullying the girls.

Ethan took the sidewalk to the main entrance at a run. Whipping open the door, he hurried along the corridor toward the office. Anxiety churned in his belly.

This wasn't his first trip to a principal's office. Not by far. He and every principal from elementary to high school had been more than mere acquaintances.

In hindsight, he realized he'd acted out to get attention. With a deadbeat father and an absentee mother, he'd figured even bad attention was better than no attention. And unfortunately, Grandma Hicks had too often been the designated adult on retrieval duty. Thanks to the Marines and Dwight Fleming, he hadn't landed where he'd been headed—jail or worse.

Time to repay the favor—to Dwight's granddaughters.

Ready to do battle, he stalked inside. Reaching for a ringing phone, the receptionist pointed to the left. He pivoted toward the row of chairs against the wall.

The twins and another child about Lucy and Stella's age huddled in three red leather armchairs.

At the sight of him, Lucy dissolved into silent sobs and hid her face in her arm. A tear rolled down Stella's stoic features. Her small hands white-knuckle gripped the armrests. All three girls looked chastened and sorrowful.

His heart broke in two. "Lucy. Stella." He went down on his knee in front of them.

Lucy looked up, her eyes red-rimmed and puffy. "I sowee, Efan," she whispered.

An older woman he presumed to be Principal Stallings emerged from an adjacent office.

He turned to the girls. "What happened?"

Lucy started to cry again and squeezed her eyes shut.

Scooping her out of the chair, he sat down, depositing Lucy in his lap. Burying her face in his shirt, she clung to him.

"Help me understand, Stella." He placed his other arm around Stella's shoulders, but she remained stiff and unresponsive. "Please tell me the truth. I won't be angry. I promise."

"Michaela said Lucy and me couldn't go to the dance tonight." Stella jabbed her finger at the other child. "Because we don't have a daddy…" Her chin quivered. "Th-that nobody loved us because we were bad girls."

The other girl studied the floor.

At the sheer cruelty of the words, he grappled with the fury rising within him. But he reminded himself the child had probably only repeated something she'd heard at home from adults. He felt a fierce protectiveness toward Amber's daughters.

Principal Stallings held out her hand to the other child. "Michaela, why don't you wait for your mother in my office?"

The pale, too-skinny little redhead hopped off the chair and took the principal's hand. Mrs. Stallings escorted her down the hall, and ushered the child inside.

Her eyes brimming, Stella peered at him. "Is it true? Are we bad girls, Ethan?"

Red-hot anger sizzled through his veins at the pain and confusion in her eyes. A pain he knew firsthand.

The sense of displacement with which he'd struggled his entire life. Of not belonging anywhere and to anyone.

He wouldn't allow that to happen to them. Not his beautiful, intelligent, warmhearted girls.

"You and Lucy are not bad." He placed his hand over her small one. "You are good, sweet girls." For the first time, Stella didn't shrink from his touch.

Principal Stallings rejoined them. "It was inexcusable what Michaela said to them. Due to privacy issues, I cannot fully disclose the details of her personal situation, but she was acting out in regards to an ongoing family crisis."

"I hit Michaela first, Mrs. Stallings." Stella lifted her chin. "It was my fault, not Lucy's."

Sniffling, Lucy raised her head. "No, Stehwaa... My fawt, too."

Mrs. Stallings's lips pursed. "I appreciate your honesty, Stella, but when Michaela hit you, Lucy hit Michaela back."

"In defense of her sister," Ethan growled.

Mrs. Stallings's eyebrow rose.

He pressed his lips together. Although his impulse was to lash out at anyone who dared to hurt them, he needed to remember he was the adult here.

God, I could use a little help in the anger and forgiveness departments.

He took a deep breath. "I'm sorry, Mrs. Stallings."

The principal's gaze bored first into Stella and then Lucy. "I hope your time away from school this afternoon will cause both of you to reflect on your behavior and on our conversation about how you might have responded differently."

Glum-faced, the girls nodded.

Mrs. Stallings laid her palm briefly on each girl's head. "We'll consider the matter settled. I look forward to seeing you both Monday morning for a new day of happy learning. Thank you for coming, Mr. Green."

A distraught woman pushed into the office. "My daughter…"

Principal Stallings moved toward the check-in counter. Rising, Ethan set Lucy on her feet. He held out his hand to Stella. Eyes downcast, she slid off the chair and twined her fingers in his.

Once outside the building, he crouched in front of the girls. "No matter what anyone says to you, it is always wrong to hurt other people." His gaze cut between Lucy and Stella. "Will you promise me that if something like this ever happens again, you'll tell a teacher? Do you promise you will not hit anyone ever again?"

"I pwomise, Efan."

His eyes darted to Stella.

"I promise, too." She bit her lip. "Do we have to tell Mommy what happened at school today?"

"We don't keep secrets from Mommy," he said.

Lucy sighed. "But she'll be so mad."

Through upswept lashes, Stella gave him a look. "You shouldn't worry Mommy, Ethan. She needs to study."

He almost laughed before he caught himself. Clever, clever Stella. Still waters *did* run deep.

"I'm not going to tell her. You two are going to tell her."

Their faces fell.

"But I'll talk to her, too."

Lucy swiped the tears off her cheek. "Is it t-woo nobody wuvs us, Efan?"

He drew both girls into an embrace. "Of course it's not true. Your mommy loves you more than anything in the whole world."

"That's wight." Lucy's head bobbed. "Mommy does wuv us, Stehwaa."

Stella looked at him. "And Gigi?"

He pulled them closer. "Gigi loves you, too."

Lucy's mouth curved. "And Maisie." She opened her hands. "Maisie wuvs us, Stehwaa."

He smiled and ticked off additional names on his fingers. "And Callie and Jake. Uncle Matt."

Lucy tucked her head into his neck.

"And me." He kissed her hair. "I love you, Lucy." He locked gazes with her sister. "I love you, Stella."

Somehow when he wasn't looking, he'd come to not only care for Amber's children but also to love them. Not what he'd imagined when he took on the task of twin-sitting. Yet here he was—his heart in the sole custody of these two little girls.

How could he make this painful day better for them?

"Girls…" He cleared his throat, hoping to dislodge the sudden boulder in his throat. "I know I'm not your father…"

How to say this? *God, help. Please.* "Girls, I'd really like to go to the dance tonight."

Lucy straightened. Stella frowned.

"And it would make me so happy if you two would come with me so I wouldn't have to go alone."

Excitement flared in Lucy's face. She'd been talking about the dance for days, but the light dimmed in her sky-blue eyes as she searched her sister's face. "Stehwaa, what do you fink?"

Stella would be the hard sell. Their incredible twin loyalty to each other was one of the things he loved most about them. He held his breath. Lucy probably did, too.

"Okay," Stella whispered. "Let's go."

Lucy broke into clapping. A weight lifted from Ethan's

shoulders. Lasting until Lucy went still and said, "But we don't have a pwincess dress to wear to the party, Efan."

And the enormity of what he'd just committed himself to hit him square between the eyes. So he did the only sensible thing he could think to do—he speed-dialed his grandmother.

"Grandma." He breathed into the phone. "I need your help."

It had been one thing after another all day.

First, the busy breakfast crowd segued without pause into a standing-room-only lunch. Then the dishwasher conked out. And a pipe burst.

Her shift ended before Amber had time to check her phone. She discovered the message she'd missed from the principal. One glance at the clock confirmed the school day had ended, and the administration had probably left the office, as well.

Panicked, she called ErmaJean, but no one answered. Rushing out the door, she scrambled into her old car. She practically flew the short distance to the Green bungalow. Getting out, she dashed up the steps.

Leaning on a crutch, ErmaJean met her at the door.

"The girls—"

"Are fine. I didn't catch the phone earlier. I don't move as fast as I used to." ErmaJean stumped toward her chair. "Come in."

Heartbeat accelerated, Amber stumbled inside. The house smelled of fresh-baked sugar cookies. "Where are they? Are they with Ethan?"

A thump sounded upstairs.

ErmaJean smiled. "No… Not with Ethan."

"I only just checked my cell. Principal Stallings left a message about what happened at school."

Leaving the crutch propped against the arm, Erma-Jean transferred to her chair. "Ethan picked them up."

So then where was he? Amber had parked beside ErmaJean's sedan. *Probably swanning about on that dumb motorcycle.*

The older woman was getting around much easier of late. But Amber didn't have time to think about that. Not now. Not when she'd rather be furious with Erma-Jean's grandson.

Of all the irresponsible... Amber planted her hands on her hips.

"So Ethan picked them up from school and then dumped them on you." She gritted her teeth. "What happened to our arrangement? His promise to take care of the girls while I was at work so you could recover?"

This is what comes from trusting men, Amber fumed. Ethan, in particular.

ErmaJean eased back in the chair. "Ethan has been with them the whole day. Me, too. We actually had a lovely afternoon. He was on the phone earlier, and then he left. He said he needed to take the Harley for a last-minute errand."

An excited giggle floated from the landing above. Lucy held a floral pink dress against her chest. "Hey, Mommy. Look what Efan bought me and Stehwaa."

Stella stood behind her sister, a floral lavender dress dragging in her hand.

"What's going on, Miss ErmaJean?" Amber hissed. "This is how Ethan responds to a serious behavioral issue with the girls? By rewarding them?"

"Mommy. Mommy," Lucy called. "Awen't I bee-you-ti-ful?"

Amber glared at the older woman.

ErmaJean shook her head. "Answer your daughter and get the facts before you skyrocket into orbit."

"Mommy?" Lucy's voice quavered.

She swallowed her indignation. "You are beautiful, Lucy. Always."

Lucy grinned. "Stehwaa and me awe going to be pwincesses at de dance with Efan."

"Dance? But…but—"

"Sit down, Amber dear, and close your mouth before you attract flies. Girls? Come tell your mommy what happened at school." She patted Amber's hand. "Try not to be too hard on them. Ethan had a long talk with them. They are very sorry, and I don't think it will ever happen again."

There were tears—not just the girls'—as they explained the events of that morning. Hugging the twins, Amber sent them upstairs to gather their belongings.

"I'd hoped they were still young enough not to be bothered by their lack of a father," she whispered.

ErmaJean's face clouded. "The moment they started school, it was inevitable they'd notice other children had fathers but they did not."

Amber put her head in her hands. "I've tried so hard to be everything to them, Miss ErmaJean."

"Only God can be everything, sweet pea. A lesson I learned early with Ethan. You do what you can, and learn to leave the rest to God." ErmaJean blew out a breath. "God is faithful. My Ethan in Truelove talking to God again is proof He is more than sufficient when we are insufficient."

"I pray so, Miss ErmaJean. Oh, how I pray it is so. But about this Sweetheart Dance…" She grimaced.

"The dance is important to the girls. Please let them go

with Ethan." ErmaJean paused as if weighing her words. "It's important to him, too."

"But the dresses." Amber gestured toward the stairs. "They look expensive."

Miss ErmaJean dipped her chin. "They were. We spent the afternoon at an Asheville department store."

"Ethan drove the girls an hour away to buy party dresses?"

"I went, too." ErmaJean's lips plumped. "He needed fashion advice."

"Even if I was to allow the girls to go with him to the Sweetheart Dance, I can't allow them to accept those dresses." She flushed. "I will not be an object of pity."

His grandmother's brow arched. "What Ethan feels for you and the girls is far from pity."

"What do you— Never mind." She waved her hand. "I can't afford those dresses, and I will not be a charity case."

ErmaJean leaned forward. "Please reconsider, Amber. Let the girls keep the dresses. They are so happy, and it made Ethan happy to buy them for Lucy and Stella. It wasn't a financial hardship for him. He has a healthy bank account." Her lips twisted. "Especially after that last no-good girlfriend of his deserted him. Good riddance to her, though. She was never good enough for him."

"As if you'd think anyone would ever be good enough for him, Miss ErmaJean."

The older woman's mouth curved. "I can think of someone good enough for him. Just right, in fact."

Amber didn't like the twinkle gleaming in ErmaJean's eyes. Too late, she remembered she was dealing with a Truelove Matchmaker. Gulping, she decided she wouldn't touch that with a ten-foot pole.

"I'm sure Lucy wants to go to this dance, but what about Stella?"

As if on cue, her more serious-minded daughter tromped downstairs. School bag slung on her shoulder, Stella also carried a large turquoise bag bearing the name of a regional department store. "We'll be so pretty, Mommy."

She smiled, and Amber's heart sank. She'd had to deny her children so much other children took for granted. And for once, she didn't have to—thanks to Ethan.

Amber couldn't find it within herself to refuse them. She wouldn't allow her pride to get in the way of her daughters' happiness. "Okay…" She sagged. "Just this once."

Lucy clambered down the stairs. "Yay!"

"Hooray!" Stella fist-pumped the air.

"Ethan said he'll pick up the girls at your house at five thirty." ErmaJean gave Amber a broad smile. "Since it's Friday night and no classes, you'll have the evening to yourself for once. Perhaps you can get a jump start on studying for your licensing exam."

She herded her daughters toward the door. "Maybe so."

But instead of elation at the prospect of her unaccustomed time off, she envisioned the long evening stretching lonely and empty before her.

A fitting metaphor for her life.

Chapter Eight

At the sound of a vehicle, Amber twitched aside the curtain in the girls' bedroom. The navy blue truck appeared vaguely familiar, but before she could puzzle it out, she spotted Ethan behind the wheel.

She let the curtain fall in place. "Prince Charming's here."

"I look silly." Stella frowned at herself in the bureau mirror. "Is my hair supposed to look fluffy on the top?"

Amber bit back a sigh. She'd spent the last two hours braiding the girls' hair into coronets. Now everyone was a critic.

"Where's my shoe? Where's my bwacelet?" Lucy hopped around the small bedroom on one foot. "We're not weady yet!"

A foreshadowing of the adolescent years to come?

Leaving them to their last-minute preparations—who knew four-year-olds had last-minute preparations?—Amber hurried to open the door. She caught Ethan, hand in midair, preparing to knock.

"Oh, hey." He let his hand fall. "Are the girls ready?"

But she couldn't take her eyes off him. A perfect fit, the gray suit outlined his broad shoulders and narrow waist. The blue oxford shirt brought out the gold flecks in his hazel eyes. And the lavender-gray striped tie provided a jaunty spring accent.

He pulled at his cuff. "Is it that bad?"

Blinking, she realized she'd taken too long to answer. "Not at all." To her chagrin, her voice had gone hoarse. "Y-you clean up pretty well." She cleared her throat.

The understatement of the year.

He smiled, lines crinkling from his eyes. "Some people, present company in particular, don't have to clean up to be pretty."

Blushing, she reminded herself to breathe. "Th-thank you, Ethan." She played with her earring, wishing she'd changed out of her usual jeans. "You are as charming as ever."

His brow creased. "I'm not trying to be charming. I just wish you could see yourself—"

"You're early."

Why was her heart thumping so?

"Better early than late." He gave her an enigmatic grin. "Who says leopards can't change their spots?"

She put her hand to her throat. That almost sounded as if he were talking about her and him. About them. But there had never been a them.

Amber bit her lip. Nor was there any likelihood there ever would be. *He's leaving in a month.* She needed to keep telling herself that until she quieted the treacherous yearnings Ethan Green seemed to bring out in her.

"We're weady!"

Amber winced. Ethan laughed.

"Lucy doesn't seem able to speak in any decibel lower than a foghorn. If you're ready," Amber called over her shoulder, "don't keep Ethan waiting, girls."

Stella stepped past her mother and onto the front porch. "Lucy says for y'all to pay attention."

Amber and Ethan exchanged amused glances.

She shook her head. "Such a drama queen."

He smiled. "Lucy is her perfectly delightful self. And I wouldn't have her any other way."

Amber wouldn't, either, but she was pleased he could see through the brash impetuousness to her daughter's sweet, kind heart. Not many people did. Not many people took the time, but Ethan had.

Throwing her arms wide, Lucy flung herself onto the porch. "Ta-da!"

Moving to the step below, he immediately dropped to one knee. *"Oh, you beautiful girls,"* he sang in a pleasing but rusty baritone. *"You great big beautiful girls."*

It was a variation of an old song Amber's dad used to sing to her mom.

Ethan placed his hand on his chest. *"Let me put my arms around you… I could never live without you…"*

Lucy struck a pose.

Amber rolled her eyes. "She's not the only ham."

"Oh, you beautiful girls." He opened his hands. *"You great big beautiful girls…"*

Amber's lips curved. "Careful you don't set the wildlife howling."

Ethan ignored her. *"If you ever leave me how my heart will ache. I want to hug you."* He angled to include Stella. *"But I fear you'd break."*

Stella scowled, dimming some of the enthusiasm in his eyes, but he rallied.

"Oh, oh, oh." Getting to his feet, he reached into a large bag he'd stashed beside the railing and removed two plastic boxes. *"Oh, you beautiful girls."* Finishing

with a flourish, he took a bow, holding the containers out to the girls.

Lucy came down a few steps and took one of the boxes from him. "What is it?"

Amber's breath hitched. "You bought each of them a corsage, Ethan?" Moisture welled in her eyes.

"A wrist corsage. Thought it would be easier for them to wear." When Stella made no move to come forward, he handed Amber the other box.

He helped Lucy remove the diminuitive cluster of pink sweetheart roses, baby's breath and purple statice from the box.

"It's so pwitty," Lucy breathed, clapping her hands to her face. "Is it for me?"

"For you." He gave Amber an uncertain smile. Very un-Ethan-like. "I hope that was okay. Every princess should have flowers when she goes to the ball, right?"

Unable to speak, she nodded.

He helped Lucy slip the elastic band over her tiny wrist.

"Wook at me, Mommy." Lucy waved her arm in the air. "I'm a weal pwincess now. Thank you, thank you, Efan."

"You're welcome, Lucy Lou." He looked at Amber. "Maybe you should help Stella."

His thoughtfulness in trying to make the evening special for her daughters nearly undid Amber. With trembling fingers, she took out Stella's corsage.

"The flowers match their dresses." He shuffled his feet on the step. "Pink and purple. For the pink and purple princesses."

Stella held out her arm. Once Amber fitted the corsage onto Stella, her daughter brought the flowers to her nose and inhaled.

A pleased expression flitted across Stella's lips. "Thank you, Ethan."

Proud she hadn't had to prompt the girls to remember their manners, Amber gave both girls a quick hug. Lucy was exuberant with her love, while Stella was more restrained with hers. But Amber detected a softening in Stella's posture that hadn't been there.

So much had changed for the better since he came into their lives. Including Amber. With each passing day, the darkness of the past faded a bit more. She felt like the sun had finally come out from the clouds and shone for the first time in a long while.

"And last but not least." He whipped out a small wildflower bouquet bound with a burlap ribbon. "For another beautiful girl." There was a shyness in his gaze as her eyes caught his. "Who became a beautiful woman and wonderful mother."

She clasped the flowers. "Ethan. You shouldn't have." The clean fragrance of meadowsweet wafted. "But thank you." Those traitorous weak tears blurred her vision. "No one has ever..."

He cocked his head. "What's wrong with the men in Truelove?"

None of them were you.

She sucked in a breath. Where had that come from? She hid her face in the sunflower-studded arrangement, giving herself time to recover her equilibrium.

"They are your favorites, right?" He propped his foot on the step between them. "Yellows. Purples and pinks. Like the meadow near the rafting office."

She looked at him. "You remember the flowers in the meadow that summer?"

"I remember a lot of things." He straightened, his face becoming serious. "Things I should've recalled sooner."

"Better late than never," she whispered.

His eyes bored into hers. "Do you mean that, Amber?" He leaned forward. Her lips parted.

In that instant, it felt to her as if the rest of the world fell away. There was no dilapidated trailer. No broken relationships. No wasted, lost years.

Only her and Ethan. The fulfillment of her schoolgirl longings. These last couple weeks, more than physical distance between them had lessened; the emotional distance had, too.

"Mommy! Efan!"

Amber jolted. Heat creeping up her neck, she pulled back.

With a sheepish look, he ran his hand over his head. "Looks like these two princesses are ready for their magical night."

Calling their goodbyes, the girls clattered after him toward the truck. And she went inside, her pulse pounding; her heart jerking.

So was she. She leaned her forehead against the closed door. *Dearest God, so am I.*

It was the perfect night for the outdoor gala. Organizers had strung twinkling lights around the perimeter of the town square. Against the backdrop of the rose-streaked sunset, a local bluegrass band performed on the raised platform of the gazebo.

Lucy was giddy with excitement. As they made their way across the lawn, Stella stuck close to his other side. Tall, thick candles in glass hurricane globes flickered on the white tables set for eight.

It was with no small relief Ethan spotted familiar faces—Jake McAbee, with his daughter, Maisie, in his arms, and Nash Jackson.

Lucy and Stella ran forward. "Maisie! Maisie!" Jake set three-year-old Maisie on her feet, and the girls admired each other's fancy dresses.

Jake shook Ethan's hand. "I'm so glad you convinced Amber to let the twins attend."

Nash nodded. "Jake and I offered, but she said she didn't want to intrude on our father-daughter moments." He grinned as Callie approached. "And though Lorena is at the hospital tonight, I'm looking forward to dinner with the best daughter in the world."

Jake placed his hand on Maisie's head. "Me, too." He winked at Callie. "I've got more than one best gal here tonight."

Callie's mouth curved. Something tender passed between them. And for the first time, Ethan felt its absence in his own life.

"As the official photographer for the gala, Amber made me promise to take lots of pictures." Callie gestured toward Dwight Fleming, standing alone near the bandstand. "I wish she and her father could've come together tonight."

So did Ethan. No diploma or nursing license would erase the heavy load she carried. He feared Amber would never find the peace she so desperately craved. Not until she reconciled with her father.

Nash clamped a hand on Ethan's shoulder. "How about your crew and my crew sit together at dinner?"

"Sounds good."

Jake took Maisie's hand. "We already claimed a table over there."

"But before your two honey bunnies get rumpled..." Callie beckoned toward the makeshift photography station. "Let's get those photos. You're my last clients before dinner."

Callie had a way of bringing out the best in her photography subjects. She did one of the three of them together. Then individual pictures of Ethan with each of the girls. She also took a sisters-only shot.

"Okay," Callie directed, the viewfinder pressed to her face. "Last picture. Act as silly as you can." She tilted her head. "Not going to be hard for the Ethan Green I remember."

He laughed. "You wound me, old friend."

"Who are you calling *old*?"

Lucy needed no encouragement to clown around. And when he obliged Callie by making fish faces, Ethan managed to coax a slight smile from Stella.

Callie gave them a thumbs-up. "Perfect!"

Lucy tugged on his sleeve. "Can we eat now, Efan?"

Callie replaced the cap on the lens of her camera. "Looks like Jake and Dad have the same idea."

Ethan steered the twins toward the buffet line. With Jake supervising Maisie, Callie was free to help him get through the line with his girls.

Temporarily his to enjoy, but lately thoughts of sandy beaches and ocean waves held less and less allure.

Juggling their plates, they started the trek across the green toward their table. Lucy and Stella adamantly refused to let him carry theirs, and then Lucy stumbled.

He made a quick grab for Lucy's plate. "Let me, Luce."

"Okay, Efan." She skipped ahead.

Stella plowed onward, resolute in her determination to do it by herself.

He helped the girls into their seats. In the beginning, he'd been optimistic he'd eventually charm his way past Stella's barriers. Amber's, too. But mother and daughter continued to hold him at arm's length.

Discouragement assailed him. And suddenly, he

doubted if he'd ever gain their trust. He'd felt something on the porch earlier between him and Amber. But it had been brief.

At the table, the Jackson-McAbee four, plus Ethan's three, left only one seat unspoken for.

Dwight pulled out the remaining chair next to Lucy. "Is this seat taken?"

The adults fell silent. The children chattered among themselves, unaware of the sudden tension.

"I don't know if you should." Ethan exchanged a look with Callie. "Amber probably wouldn't like it."

The older man's face fell. "I just wanted to be close to them, but I don't want to cause any trouble."

Lucy's head popped up from the meatball she was jabbing with a blue toothpick. "Mi-kay-waa's mom said Stehwaa and me awe double twouble."

"Not double trouble." Dwight's blue eyes—so similar to his granddaughters'—sparked. "Double blessing."

Emotion clogged Ethan's throat. This wasn't right. Keeping Dwight from knowing his granddaughters. Denying Lucy and Stella the opportunity to know their grandfather.

"Take the seat, Dwight," his voice rasped. "We'd be glad to have you join us."

"If you're sure." Dwight looked around the table at the sea of faces. Callie gave a slow nod. Nash, too.

Later, clutching her camera, Callie excused herself when the mayor mounted the dais to speak. He and other Truelove personages gave short updates on the progress of the fund-raising effort to outfit the high school band with new uniforms. Seated toward the rear of the crowd, the three little girls whispered among themselves.

"Your grandmother called me this afternoon." Driven by a stark hunger to know them, Dwight's gaze remained focused on his granddaughters. "She mentioned you were escorting the girls to the dance tonight."

Grandma Hicks. Ethan should've guessed. The matchmakers were notorious for rushing in where sensible folk feared to tread.

"So you came to the Sweetheart Dance just to see them, Dwight?"

Dwight's gaze darted to Ethan. "I did." Grief—over his dead wife and over Amber—had clearly aged him, etching sorrow upon his rugged features.

Across the table, Nash leaned forward. "It's not right this breach between family members. Nor among believers." The flame of the candle flared. "I've told Amber Dawn so. But she's stubborn."

Dwight's mouth pursed. "Like her father."

"There is that." Nash placed his palms flat on the tablecloth. "But I've not given up on the Lord softening her heart to you. I'm in faith believing through God's sovereignty that all things work for good for those who love Him."

All things? Ethan stared at the flickering flame inside the glass lantern. His dad leaving? Lucy and Stella not having a father? He didn't see how any of that could work out for anyone's good, much less his own.

Dwight shook his head. "It's my fault for what happened."

Nash steepled his hands. "But where would any of us be without the grace of the Father's forgiveness to us?"

Lucy turned toward Dwight. "My name is Woocy." She motioned to her sister. "Her name's Stehwaa." She tilted her blond head. "What's your name?"

"Dwight." His Adam's apple bobbed in his throat. "Dwight Fleming."

Ethan froze the instant he said it.

"Fweming?" Lucy laughed. "Isn't dat funny, Stehwaa? We have de same name as him."

Jake studied the tablecloth. Nash shuffled his feet. Dwight threw Ethan an apologetic look.

Speeches over, the band burst into a lively folk tune, and Lucy almost turned her chair over trying to get out of the seat. "I wuv dis song!" She pulled at Ethan's arm. "Let's dance, Efan. Come on. I show you."

He paused beside Stella. "Do you want to dance, too?"

She pursed her lips. "No, thank you."

Jake rose to dance with Maisie. Leaving Stella in Nash's care, Ethan allowed himself to be towed to the small dance floor. Lucy's dancing was more function than form. Like everything else in her young life, she threw herself into dancing with a hearty gusto. He soon realized that all he had to do was to stand still and let Lucy gyrate around him as if he were a maypole.

It was slightly funny. Okay, it was hilarious. Smiling at him, the other couples carefully skirted around Lucy's flailing limbs. Their warmth took him aback. He wasn't used to being on the receiving end of Truelove approval.

He could get used to this. Ethan frowned. Too used to feeling as if he belonged. He reminded himself he couldn't wait to be shed of this one-stoplight town. The sooner, the better.

Ethan glanced at the bebopping Lucy. Although that would mean leaving the girls, too. And Amber. His heart shrank at the prospect. Leaving him second-guessing himself.

Which he hated.

After the song ended, Nash claimed Lucy for the next dance. Ethan sat with Maisie and Stella so Jake could dance with his wife.

Ever bold, Lucy touched Dwight's arm. "Where's your daughter, Mr. Fweming?"

A mist enveloped his eyes. "She—she couldn't be here with me tonight, sweetheart."

Lucy smiled. "I have a gweat idea… Efan doesn't need two pwincesses. I can be your pwincess for dis dance, Mr. Fweming. Would you wike dat?"

Dwight's chin wobbled. "I'd like that so much, Lucy." He swallowed. "If that's all right with you, Ethan?"

In for a penny, in for a pound.

Ethan nodded.

Delighted, Lucy led the grandfather she didn't know she had to the dance pavilion. Leaving Ethan and Stella alone at the table. He examined his watch. It was long past the girls' usual bedtime. At least tomorrow was Saturday.

The band segued into an old-fashioned waltz. Gazing at the milling crowd, Stella appeared small in the white fold-up chair. He should think about getting the girls home to Amber.

He'd risen to his feet to call Lucy when an inexplicable urge to ask Stella to dance one more time overcame him. Here went nothing but—

"Stella, you don't have to if you don't want to…" He held out his hand. "But would you like to dance with me?"

The candle cast a glow on her face. Her gaze pingponged from his hand to his face and back again. Well, at least he'd tried.

She edged out of her chair. "Okay."

He blinked at her for a second before gathering his wits. "Great. Fantastic. Marvelous."

Slipping her hand in his, she shook her head, but a smile played on her small lips. "Don't oversell it, Ethan."

He laughed, the resemblance between Stella and her mother never sharper.

Once on the dance floor, however, she faltered.

"I don't know how to do this dance," she whispered.

Ethan bit the inside of his cheek. "I'm not much of a dancer, either, but Gigi did make me learn this one." He took both of her hands. "How about you step on my feet and I'll move for both of us?"

He hardly felt her weight. "This is called a waltz, Stella. I can remember sometimes Gigi and my grandfather used to dance in the kitchen."

A sweet memory he hadn't recalled until now. How his grandmother must miss his granddad. He sure did.

Concentrating on not falling off his shoes, Stella bit her lip.

"If you can count to four, you can do the waltz, Stella."

She jutted her chin. "I can count to a hundred."

He smiled. "You are a smart girl. When I was your age I could only count to zero."

She rolled her eyes at him. He smiled. Seeing more and more of her mother. The best of her mother.

"That's silly, Ethan."

"For a waltz, you only need to count to four. Help me count, okay?" He winked. "In case I still get my numbers confused."

That earned him a smile. A small smile. But hey, he'd take what he could get when it came to Stoic Stella.

"Here we go. One…" Holding her hands, he glided left. "Two…" He slid forward. "Three…" Back where they'd begun. "We make a box."

She peered at him, a quizzical look on her face.

"A square."

"I know about squares and triangles." She cocked

her head. "I know about octagons, too, although I can't spell it."

"Can't spell it *yet*, you very smart girl, you."

She smiled, a real one this time. And he felt able to slay dragons. Able to leap tall buildings in a single bound.

"One. Two. Three." He twirled her on his feet around the dance floor, just to show her off. "One. Two. Three."

Her eyes lighting up, she waved at the astonished Lucy before she remembered she needed to hold on to his hands. Eyes widening, she teetered. Ethan caught her arm just in the nick of time.

The waltz, which was the last song of the evening, ended. He brought Stella to the table. Callie made a point of congratulating her on learning a new dance. Lucy poked out her lips.

He tweaked the tip of her nose. "Next waltz is for you." And then remembered there would be no next Sweetheart Dance for him. Next year this time, he'd be in Wilmington. Amber, Lucy and Stella would be far, far away here in Truelove.

His stomach clenched.

Was he making a mistake?

Chapter Nine

Every few minutes—Amber couldn't seem to help herself—she got off the couch and checked the driveway for signs of their return.

Restless, she found herself unable to concentrate on studying. Instead, she scrolled through the photos that Callie had emailed of the girls and Ethan. The picture of Stella standing on Ethan's shoes while they danced reduced her to tears. They looked so sweet together. So right.

The way it should've always been for her girls. With a father who loved them enough to stick around, good times or bad. She mourned for the special father-daughter bond she'd once shared with her dad. Her heart ached for the fatherly love the twins had been denied. For all the future father-daughter moments they'd likely never know.

Impatient with herself, she swiped away the tears. Aside from the love she lavished on her girls, she'd spent the last five years in a state of self-imposed numbness. Because when Tony abandoned them, she'd lost more than a husband.

She'd lost her self-confidence. Her self-esteem. Worst

of all, her belief in finding personal happiness. Her girlish daydreams of love had been ground to dust.

Thereafter, she'd resolved to focus her energy—both physical and emotional—on her children and nursing school. Yet ever since Ethan returned, she'd been feeling tendrils of hope springing forth in the soil of her heart once again.

And that was an invitation to disaster.

She couldn't afford hope. The loss of it was simply too devastating to bear. Better to root it out now. To confine herself to practicalities.

It was after nine when she finally heard the whine of an engine. She hurried onto the porch as Ethan shut off the motor and got out of the truck. She'd meant to ask him where he'd gotten the truck...

Tie loosened, collar unbuttoned, Ethan came around the hood. "We're back."

He gave her that ridiculously heart-quivering, knee-buckling smile of his, and she was struck momentarily speechless. When he wasn't around, she told herself she must disremember him being so handsome. Yet the next time she saw him, she realized afresh she hadn't recalled even the half of it. Or maybe it was just her he affected so.

Ethan opened the cab door. "A good time, I think, was had by all."

Both girls lay, heads back, zonked out in their booster seats.

"It looks like you did." She hugged her arms around herself. "Callie sent photos. And you've managed to perform quite a feat—wearing my girls out."

He grinned. "I aim to please."

Amber's heart lurched. Ethan Green did please. Oh, so much.

Stella's eyes popped open. "Mommy?" She stretched out her arms.

"Hey, honey." Amber smiled. "Did you have a good time at the dance?"

Ethan unfastened the booster seat buckle.

Nodding, Stella rubbed her eyes. "I wish you had come to the dance with us."

Amber bit her lip. She wished she could've been there, too. Images of the four of them being together flashed into her mind. Callie taking fun family pictures of her, Ethan and the girls.

Crazy, impossible dreams. *Stop it, Amber.*

Lifting Stella from the car seat, he handed her to Amber. Laying her head on her mother's shoulder, Stella's arms went around Amber's neck. She breathed in the sweet scent of her child.

This was real, Amber reminded herself. Stella, Lucy and her. The rest was only a bittersweet, never to be attained illusion.

He freed an unresponsive Lucy from her seat. "I'll carry her inside." Cradling Lucy's inert form against his chest, he winked at Amber. "Maybe they'll sleep until noon."

"Not going to happen." Lips quirking, she led the way into the house. "The girls get up before the chickens."

She stepped aside, allowing him to pass. "If you wouldn't mind laying Lucy on her bed, I'd appreciate it."

"No problem."

Closing the door, she shifted Stella to her other hip and followed him down the hall. Her girls were getting too big to carry—moments like this would soon come to an end. Stumbling behind him, her eyes watered.

She blinked the moisture away. It wasn't like her to

be so emotional. The fatigue of her daily grind must be catching up to her.

Using his shoulder, he flicked the light switch on their bedroom wall. He scanned the white painted dresser and the cheerful quilts that covered the two small beds.

"Their room is just as it should be." He glanced over his shoulder at her. "Did Grandma make the quilts for them?"

"Yes. She's become such an important person in our lives. Thank you so much for not making her leave Truelove. I don't know what we would do without her." Amber choked up.

He looked away as if her words made him uncomfortable. "Which bed is Lucy's?"

She gestured to the one on the left.

Ethan laid Lucy on top of the covers, and she immediately curled into a ball. He stuck his hands in his trouser pockets. "I guess I should go."

Amber's heart pounded. She didn't want him to go. Not yet.

"Ladies need their beauty sleep." His eyes cut to hers. "N-not you, though." Red crept from beneath the starched collar of his blue shirt. "I—I mean, because you've already got plenty of beauty," he stammered.

Amber's heart quickened. "You think I'm beautiful?"

His face softened. "I've always thought you were beautiful."

Their gazes locked.

"If you're not in a hurry, maybe you could wait while I get the girls settled." Hiding a blush, she set Stella on her bed. "I'd like to get them into their pajamas, but I think teeth-brushing will have to be put off until morning." Her heart in her throat, she angled. "Stay. Unless there's somewhere else you need to be."

They shared a long look.

"I can't think of a single place I'd rather be than here, Amber." He swallowed. "With you."

He headed toward the living room, and she helped Stella slip into her pajamas. Limp as a wet rag, getting Lucy changed was like dressing a jellyfish. Amber tucked her between the sheets.

"Efan…" Lucy murmured. "Where's Efan, Mommy?"

Stella flipped aside the quilt. "I need to tell him something."

"Don't get out of bed, Stella. I'll get him."

Amber hurried down the hall. Holding the framed photo of the twins' on their fourth birthday, he looked up at the sound of her footfalls on the carpet.

"The girls want to say good-night, Ethan."

He set down the picture. "Sure."

When they returned to the small bedroom, the girls were already half-asleep and fading fast.

Yawning, Lucy tucked her hands beneath her pillow. "Night-night, Efan."

He touched his palm to her cheek. "Good night, Lucy Lou."

"I need to tell you something, Ethan," Stella whispered.

He came over to her bed. "Yes, Stella Bella?" She scooted to give him room. He sank onto the mattress beside her.

Stella fisted the covers. "I—I…"

Eyebrow raised, he exchanged a look with Amber. Positioned at the foot of the bed, Amber shrugged.

He patted Stella's leg under the quilt. "What is it, sweetheart?"

She flung her arms around his neck. "I—I love you, Ethan." Stella buried her face in the hollow of his shoulder. "Forever."

Amber held her breath.

He lifted his hands as if to embrace her, but faltered as if unsure of what he should do. Was he aware of the significance of Stella opening her heart to him? But he must have understood because after a fraction of a heartbeat, his arms went around Stella.

"I love you, too, Stella. So much." His voice was hoarse with emotion. He squeezed his eyes shut. "Forever."

Leaving Amber reeling. And wondering if she dared be as brave with her heart as her daughter.

After a quick kiss on her cheek, Ethan said good-night and left Amber to tuck Stella into bed.

He stumbled to the living room. Had that just happened? He raked his hand over his head. Slow-to-warm Stella loved him. And he felt shaken by her trust in him. With the sacred, precious treasure of her heart. An enormous responsibility. He scrubbed his face.

Everyone in Truelove knew Ethan Green was the poster child for irresponsibility. So what was he doing? What was he thinking, getting close to Lucy and Stella? Opening his heart to them?

He'd fail them. Disappoint them. Like he'd disappointed his parents and Kelly. He wasn't good with relationships. He didn't do commitment. Panicked, he would've fled—his second favorite fallback after anger—if he hadn't promised to wait for Amber.

When Amber walked into the living room, he glimpsed a raw vulnerability in her azure eyes. Uncertainty and fear flickered across her lovely face. "Ethan…"

And suddenly, more than his own fears of inadequacy, he wanted to erase her fear, her pain. He wanted to be there for her. He wanted her.

He rubbed the back of his neck. "Seems like a long time ago I promised to take you to prom."

"By the time I was old enough to go to prom, you'd joined the Marines. Donald Mills took me to prom."

Ethan frowned. "Mills the geek?"

"I would've done far better to have stuck with him instead of Tony." She pursed her lips. "Donald has done well for himself with some social media company."

Ethan held out his hand to her. "Did you save one dance for me?"

She looked from his hand to his face. "You want to dance with me? Now?"

"Am I too late to claim my dance?" So much more hung in the balance than a mere dance.

She swallowed. "There isn't any music."

"We'll make our own."

She took a step back. "We're not those same teenagers. Your life is in Wilmington. My life…" She gestured behind her. "My life is with them." She moistened her lips. "What would be the point?"

Amber was right. What would be the point in starting something neither of them were free to finish? But the yearning he'd felt since the summer he turned eighteen clamored inside him. Refusing to be deflected, distracted or denied.

He took a step forward. The urgency mounted to touch his lips to hers. To taste the sweetness, which had always been such a part of who she was. To know, if only for this brief interlude in both their lives, happiness.

"Ethan…" Her voice broke. "I'm too old to dream."

Shoving aside his doubts and misgivings, he took her in his arms. He would've backed off immediately if she'd tried to pull away, but she didn't. Instead, she placed her hands on his shoulders.

"You can't ever be too old to dream, Amber." He pulled her close. "I've dreamed of this moment for so long."

Swaying into him, she lifted her face. "You have?"

Ethan nodded. Only a fraction of an inch separated his mouth from hers. His heart jackhammering in his chest, he bent his head. He tilted his chin. His mouth found hers.

But almost as quickly he drew back, giving her the freedom to break away if she wished. Her hands interlocked behind his neck. She pulled his head toward her mouth.

"Amber…" he murmured before he kissed her again.

The sweetness he'd expected. The rush of strong feeling, however, took him by surprise. Like nothing he'd ever experienced before.

Far more than the remembered adolescent crush, this—whatever this was he felt for Amber—shook him to his core.

She trembled in his arms, and he broke off the kiss, holding her gently against his chest.

"You've got the weekend off?" he whispered into the silkiness of her hair.

He felt her breath against his neck. "I do."

He kissed her forehead. "Then let's enjoy the weekend together. What do you say?"

She searched his face for answers he couldn't provide. Finally when he believed he could bear her silence no longer…

"The girls and I come as a package, Ethan."

His arms tightened fractionally around her before he released her. "I wouldn't want it any other way."

Another surprise. But it was true. And he could hardly wait for tomorrow.

Chapter Ten

Saturday was the most fun Amber had experienced in a long time. Ethan made everything fun. All four of them went hiking in the Blue Ridge Mountains and, to the girls' delight, ran across a waterfall. He was so patient and kind with Lucy and Stella. They'd given their heart to him completely.

Driving home after a full day of adventure, the girls fell asleep in the back seat of the truck. As he pulled next to the trailer, they even didn't stir.

"Let them sleep." He cut the engine. "That way we can talk, just the two of us." He reached across the seat for her hand.

Her pulse leaping at his touch, she laced her fingers in his. "I keep meaning to ask you where you borrowed the truck."

"I didn't borrow it." He gave her a crooked smile. "I bought it."

She blinked. "You bought it?"

"Jonas Stone sold it to me. He'd already bought another vehicle for the ranch, so I bought it and sold the Harley to the dealership on the highway."

She frowned. "But you loved that ridiculous death-machine. Why did you sell your motorcycle?"

"Because…" He squeezed her hand. "My girls needed a proper carriage to go to their princess ball last night."

Amber's mouth went dry. "You sold your motorcycle and bought a truck just to take Lucy and Stella to the dance?"

Ethan shrugged. "I'd been thinking about it awhile. I wanted my own set of wheels." He looked away. "Besides, the Harley didn't work for all of us being together."

He'd sold his Harley so he could go places with her and the girls?

She wasn't sure how she should respond so she let the subject drop. Later, though, after he went home, she had plenty to say to the girls. Speaking as much for their sakes as her own.

Over the next few days, she repeatedly cautioned the girls to remember Ethan was only here temporarily until Miss ErmaJean got back on her feet. And every day, his grandmother regained more of her independence. Amber begged the girls to remember that one day soon Ethan would return to his real life, which was far away.

Best not to get too attached, she admonished. It would only make his leave-taking harder. The girls would undoubtedly miss him. She would miss him, but she'd get over it. She'd get over whatever this was between them. She had once before. She would again.

Lucy and Stella blissfully ignored her warnings.

Ethan had made her no promises. And she appreciated that about him. They'd made each other no promises. Best to not make promises you can't keep.

The next few weeks flew by. On Mother's Day, Ethan took her, the girls and Miss ErmaJean out for lunch.

Then the twins surprised her with a gift card to a big-box store.

Stella smiled. "For you, Mommy."

"Happy Moder's Day." Lucy clapped. "Efan took us shopping."

Amber's eyes stung with unshed tears. "I've never received a Mother's Day gift before."

"I decided it was about time you did." He squeezed her fingers. "I heard you've been sending out résumés and thought this might be useful."

A lump formed at the base of her throat.

They settled into an easy routine. Ethan took to dropping by the café during her lunch break. Over turkey sandwiches and sweet tea, they laughed, discovered each other's preferences on a host of topics and got to know each other again.

On Friday nights, ErmaJean insisted they leave the girls with her and go out on a real date. They held hands at the movies. One Friday, they went to the Asheville mall. After dining in the food court, they shopped for professional attire for her to wear to prospective job interviews.

"Do you think the hospital will hire you?"

She shuffled through the skirts on the garment rack. "They've expressed interest, but the hours would be hard with the girls' schedule."

He showed her a navy blue blazer.

She smiled. "I like that." She scanned the price tag. "And I like the fact that it's on clearance even better." She tilted her head. "You're pretty good at this."

He cocked his head. "That's what all my ladies tell me."

She arched her brow. "All your ladies? You have so many?"

His lips twitched. "I have four. Grandma. Stella. Lucy." He planted a quick kiss on her cheek. "And you."

But in spite of the fun of having him to herself on Fridays, her favorite times with him were Monday and Wednesday nights.

On those evenings, he joined her and the girls for dinner at her place. He insisted on bringing groceries. At first, she took offense.

"I eat more than you three put together," he said. "If you're going to feed me, I'm providing the food."

He also took it upon himself to make some much-needed repairs to the trailer.

Fresh and clean from their baths, the girls would cuddle against him on the couch. He read the library books the girls had checked out from school. Including their favorite storybook, which he'd given them to keep, the one about the ducklings that had belonged to Ethan as a child. Their little faces upturned to him as a sunflower turned itself to the rays of the sun. They adored him.

She could so very easily allow herself to fall in love with him. But of course, she wouldn't. He was leaving. She was staying.

Don't look too hard into the future, she told herself. *Just enjoy the here and now.*

On her next nonclinical Saturday, he announced it was a perfect day for a picnic. Easing back into cooking, ErmaJean supplied the fixings, and they set off.

Turning off the mountain road, he parked in a glen not far from the river. He lugged the picnic basket while the girls raced ahead to the meadow.

Billowing the blanket over the tall grass, she decided it was a perfect spring day. Like puffy cotton balls, clouds drifted lazily across a brilliant blue sky. Through the trees, the sounds of the river gurgled. Birdsong filled the air with melody. Wildflowers dotted the meadow. On the other side of the riverbank, the mountains undulated in blue-green waves on the horizon.

Seated on the blanket, she handed Stella a sandwich. "I haven't been here since I was a kid."

Leaning back, he stretched out the long length of him and closed his eyes. "Me either."

She passed the carrots to Lucy. "You're still nothing but a big oversize kid."

He grabbed a sandwich. "Good thing you like kids, eh?" He smirked.

She made sure he saw her roll her eyes.

The girls quickly finished their lunch and got up to play.

"Be careful," she called after them. "Stay where I can see you."

She repacked the basket. "I spent so many wonderful days here with you, Matt and Callie."

He opened one eye. "I remember."

She scanned the landscape for the twins. "Back then, it would've never occurred to me to worry about snakes."

"That's what being a parent does for you, I guess."

Of course, the biggest snake had been Tony. Her father and Callie had tried to warn her, but she'd been grief-stricken with the loss of her mother and too headstrong to listen.

Marry in haste. Repent at your leisure.

She glanced across the blanket to Ethan. The knot in her stomach pulled tighter. She should remember this was a pleasant, but very temporary, dream come true.

"Mommy! Efan! Come quick!" Lucy shrieked.

Heart in her throat, Amber scrambled off the blanket. Jumping to his feet, Ethan raced ahead, charging over the incline of the hill.

"Lucy! Stella!" he yelled. "Where are you?"

Dashing after him through the meadow grass, Amber berated herself for losing sight of the twins. She wasn't an adolescent girl anymore, crushing on her brother's best friend. She was a mother with responsibilities. No time for foolish flights of fancy.

Amber came to an abrupt halt on the crest of the slope. Below on the riverbank, Ethan had reached the twins, who appeared unharmed. And she realized what had caused the excitement.

Stella waved her mother forward. "Boats, Mommy." She pointed to the bright flotilla of watercrafts paddling downriver.

Relief mixing with chagrin, Amber picked her way toward the edge of the water. "Kayaks."

"Dey're so pwitty, Mommy." Lucy bounced in her sneakers. "Dey're f-whying acwoss the water."

"I want to kayak, Mommy." Stella pulled on her arm. "Can we go kayaking, Ethan?"

Scratching his head, he cut his eyes at her.

"I want de blue one." Lucy gestured.

Stella scowled at her sister. "No, I want the blue one."

"Girls," Amber said. "No one is getting the blue one. The river is not for little kids."

And then as if to completely belie her words, a canoe rounded the bend. A strawberry-blonde woman and a very handsome man maneuvered the craft between the water hazards. A small brown-haired boy about the twins' age sat between them.

Lucy's lips poked out. "He wooks wike he's having fun."

Stella planted her hands on her little hips. "You never let us have any fun, Mommy."

A refrain she—and probably every other mother on

the planet—had heard before. Mean old mom. Why does everybody else get to… Yada. Yada. Yada. The basic refrain, any time a mother kept her children from doing something they wanted.

She crossed her arms. "Not happening, girls."

They groaned. And turned their wide-eyed appeal to Ethan.

"We could do it wif Efan," Lucy said.

"Please, Mommy. Please…" Stella gave her puppy dog eyes. "Ethan would keep us safe."

"Maybe the river's in their blood," he murmured. "The Fleming legacy."

She glared at him. "That isn't funny, Ethan. Stop being such a marshmallow. The girls are working you."

Palms up, he laughed. "Can't help it. I'm a sucker for big blue Fleming eyes."

His lopsided grin sent a flutter down to her toes.

Leaning closer, his lips brushed her earlobe. "Always have been," he whispered.

She blushed.

"Wook, Mommy!" Lucy pointed to a raft full of people barreling downstream. "I know him."

Stella nodded. "He has the same name as us."

The rafting guide was her father. In the fast, flowing current, the raft soon disappeared beyond the curve of the river.

She took hold of Lucy's arm. "How do you know that man?"

Lucy tugged free. "He danced wif me."

Amber angled to Ethan. "What's she talking about?"

Suddenly, he seemed unable to meet her gaze.

"Mr. Fweming is a vewee nice man, Mommy." Lucy smiled. "Do you know him, too?"

Amber's jaw tightened. "Ethan…"

He blew out a breath. "It was no big deal. The night of the dance we were seven at a table of eight. Dwight took the last chair."

"No big deal?" she sputtered. "Why didn't you tell me?"

He stuck his hands in his pockets. "Dwight regrets what happened, Amber."

"You've had conversations with him about me?" Her voice rose.

"He only wanted to meet Lucy and Stella." Ethan tugged the back of his neck. "Dwight's lonely, Amber. He desperately wants to be close to you again. For you to be part of his life."

"If he's lonely, it's his own fault. Why would you allow him access to my girls, Ethan? You know how I feel about him." She threw out her hands. "After what he did… didn't do…when I needed him the most."

"Mommy…" Lucy's face puckered.

"Did we do something wrong?" Stella's chin wobbled. "Are we in trouble, Mommy?"

"No." She wheeled toward the slope. "But Ethan is."

"Amber." He took hold of her arm. "Wait."

"It's time to leave, girls." She jerked free. "I absolutely cannot believe you'd do this behind my back, Ethan. I trusted you to look out for them. To keep their best interests at heart."

Lucy started to cry. Scowling, Stella scuffed the ground with the toe of her sneaker, sending a pebble ricocheting into the water.

"Don't be mad wif Efan, Mommy," Lucy sobbed. "We wuv him."

"I always have their best interests at heart." He jutted his jaw. "You're being unreasonable. Your pride is misplaced. It's you who's lost sight of their best interests."

She sucked in a breath. "How dare you! You waltz into our lives and think you have the right to tell me how to raise my children? What kind of friend are you?"

His gaze hardened. "I'm the kind of friend who's willing to tell you the truth when you're making a mistake. I'm the only friend you've not cowed into silence about this issue with your father."

She lifted her chin. "I think it best if you take us home now." She glowered at him.

"Whatever happened to forgiveness, Amber?" His mouth thinned. "What kind of example—"

She fisted her hands. "I can't talk to you right now, Ethan. Take us home."

What a fool she'd been to trust him. When would she learn she couldn't trust men? She'd begun to believe he was different. But he was just like the rest. Like her father. Like Tony.

A muscle ticked in his cheek. "Have it your way. I'll get the basket and be at the truck." He stalked up the hill, disappearing into the waving meadow grass.

She stared after him in disbelief. How had this sunny, picture-perfect day dissolved into bitter words? So out of control. She wasn't the only hardheaded, unreasonable...

"Let's go, girls," she grunted.

Sniffling, Lucy headed up the embankment. Stella stomped after her sister. The drive to the trailer was accomplished in stony silence.

Amber hopped out. "Go to the house, girls."

Ethan helped them unbuckle their seats.

Easing out of the truck, Lucy blinked away tears. "I want Efan..."

Tapping her foot on the ground, Amber fumed. How had she ended up the bad guy?

Stella's mouth trembled. "When will we see Ethan again?"

"I don't know. Go." She pointed toward the trailer. "Now."

Shoulders slumped, the girls moved toward the porch.

He wrapped his hands around the frame of the truck door. "Don't punish my grandmother or the girls for my mistake. Or is it only me you plan to bar from their lives?"

Amber's chest heaved. Truth was, she needed him if she was going to finish the semester. She was so sick of having to depend on others. Of being beholden.

"Car pool as usual," she growled. "But otherwise, it would probably be better if we kept our distance."

A muscle jerked in his cheek, and he stared into the space above her head. "Whatever you say. Your choice."

"When has anything in the last five years been my choice?" She slammed the cab door shut. The truck rocked. "One wrong decision and nothing has ever been the same. Nothing has gone right for me."

Ethan's eyes glinted. "Is that so?" he said in a slow, gravelly drawl.

Her conscience pricked. Ashamed of herself, heat crept up her face. It wasn't true.

She had two healthy, wonderful children. The matchmakers and Callie had stood by her during this long season of finishing her degree. God had never forsaken her.

Cocking his head, he got behind the wheel. "Let me know when you're over this little temper tantrum of yours, Amber."

She stepped away as the truck reversed and rattled toward the road.

In truth, not merely one wrong choice. As for Ethan… Her lungs constricted. Had she just made another irreversible mistake?

* * *

Ethan didn't feel up to facing Amber at church the next day. She'd made her feelings—or the lack thereof—only too clear.

As for his feelings?

In a fury of blinding dust, he took out his ire on the tallboy dresser instead. A movement at the door of the workshop snared his attention.

He cut the sander off. "Grandma?"

"My, my," she tsk-tsked. "What did that dresser ever do to you?"

He clenched his jaw. "What're you doing out here?"

"The therapist said it was good for me to exercise. To put weight on my leg again in order to regain my strength."

"Walking around the house is one thing." He frowned. "The ground is uneven between the driveway and the workshop. You could've fallen."

"You stomped out of the kitchen this morning like a man on fire. What's going on, Ethan?"

He set the sander onto the workbench with a clatter. "You know what's going on." After storming home yesterday afternoon, he'd filled his grandmother in on what had happened at the river.

"Maybe you should call Amber and apologize."

His mouth fell open. "Apologize? She's the one—"

"Amber isn't the only one who has a problem in the pride department." His grandmother cocked her hip. "Is that why you decided for us to skip church this morning?"

He flushed. He'd hared off to the workshop without considering that his truancy meant his grandmother would miss church, as well.

"I'm sorry, Grandma." He removed his protective goggles. "I should've called Miss GeorgeAnne to come get you."

"What really concerns me is what you plan to do about this disagreement with Amber. Things were going so well between you."

He scowled. "Sorry to be the kink in your carefully laid matchmaker schemes, Grandma. As for plans? I'm sticking to the original plan."

"Which is?"

"To get us out of Truelove as soon as I can."

Grandma sighed. "I thought we had moved beyond that."

So had he. He'd actually started thinking about the possibility of putting down permanent roots in Truelove. Rebuilding his grandfather's business. Making a new life. Exploring new relationships. And then this business with Amber…

More fool he.

Women. First, Kelly. Now, Amber. They were all alike.

"Do you know what they call someone who keeps doing the same thing over and over again, expecting a different result?"

Her eyes sparked. "An optimist?"

"A chump." His mouth flattened. "And I'm tired of dancing to someone else's tune."

"Seems to me dancing is what started this whole fiasco. Perhaps if I called Amber to explain…" His grandmother's brow knotted. "I'm to blame for calling Dwight about the dance."

He snorted. "She won't listen. Her mind's made up on the subject of Dwight and so's mine."

"The both of you need time to cool off. Don't do something you'll regret."

"What I regret is ever letting you talk me into this… this *arrangement* in the first place."

"Ethan."

He widened his stance. "Three weeks until she graduates. With the cast coming off soon, only two weeks before you're released from therapy. Better wrap your head around it, Grandma, and start saying your goodbyes. I can't wait to leave this two-bit town in the dust for good."

"It's not like you to give up so easily, son. She's been hurt, badly, by every man in her life. Her anger was a knee-jerk reaction. She's working through a lot."

"Aren't we all?" He grimaced. "Face it. This deal has gone bust. Amber and I were never meant to be."

"I don't believe that's true." Turning to go, his grandmother threw him a final look. "What's more, I don't think you believe that, either. If you truly care about Amber as much as I suspect you always have, you won't allow your injured male pride to stand in the way. You'll get yourself over to Amber's and work this out like the grown-ups both of you are supposed to be."

"You overreacted, dear friend." Slipping onto the stool, Callie folded her hands on the counter at the Mason Jar. "Again."

It was Wednesday morning, and Amber had ample opportunity to regret her harsh words to Ethan. Not that she was ready to admit it out loud.

Amber narrowed her eyes at her best friend. "Don't think it has escaped my notice that you were in on this conspiracy, too."

Callie shook her head. "Do you hear yourself, Amber? There was no conspiracy. You're making far more out of this than there ever was. Dwight sat with us at dinner. That's it."

"I'm trying to protect my children."

"You're trying to protect yourself." Callie lifted her chin. "Things with Ethan were getting serious. And that scared you to death, so you did what you always do. You self-sabotage."

"That isn't true."

"Sure it is. You're just too stubborn to admit you're on the brink of what may be the best thing that ever happened to you, save Lucy and Stella."

Biting her lip, Amber stared out the window overlooking the town square.

"I've never seen you so happy, Amber. Not since…" Callie pressed her lips together.

Amber twisted the hem of her apron. This had been the happiest she'd been since maybe even before her mother died and her life had unraveled. Perhaps since Ethan left Truelove to join the Marines.

"I can't bear to think of you throwing away this opportunity for happiness." Reaching across the counter, Callie touched her hand. "Give this thing with Ethan another chance. Give yourself another chance. Y'all have been so good together with the girls." Callie got off the stool. "At least pray about it. Please."

Pray? She'd barely slept since Saturday. She'd been relieved when neither Ethan nor Miss ErmaJean had showed for church. But of all days, the reverend had chosen to preach on forgiveness. And she'd squirmed through the sermon. Amber was having a hard time getting the resounding truth of Reverend Bryant's words out of her head.

"The person who is forgiven much, loves much," the reverend had admonished his congregation. "What people don't often stop to consider is the flip side of that Biblical truth. That to the one who forgives little, the same loves little." The pastor opened his hands. "But how shameful if that should be said of us, dear brothers and sisters. For no matter what you or I have done, God in His mercy has forgiven each of us much. How, therefore, can we not do likewise with one another?"

In that moment, it felt as if God Himself had shone a spotlight on her tangled emotions.

"If God is willing to forgive your sins though they be as scarlet, why, dearest children, can you not forgive yourself?"

Her heart had pounded.

"And as long as that is the case..." Reverend Bryant's hands had gripped the pulpit. "Then I fear you will also be a person who loves little. Forever unable to receive love, as well."

The bell over the entrance jangled as Callie departed the café. With the diner almost deserted, Amber had too much time to consider the consequences of her actions.

Had she overreacted?

Needing to escape her anxious thoughts, she decided to bus the corner booth. But scraping the dirty plates, inevitably her mind strayed to the last few excruciating days.

Tuesday evening after class, Ethan had met her at the door with the sleepy, pajama-clad twins. He didn't look at her, much less speak to her. She got the impression he was as ticked off with her as she was with him.

Well, good riddance. She didn't need him. She and the girls had been doing fine before he showed up.

That wasn't true. None of them had been doing fine. Especially her.

Exams were starting next week. She rubbed her forehead. She didn't need this added stress in her life. So much rested on the outcome of her scores. She had an interview for a job in a few days.

She'd come so far. She'd hoped, but never allowed herself to dream, this opportunity with Truelove's new pediatrician might come her way. Though she knew what Ethan would have said to that. That she didn't dream enough.

Working at the pediatric office would mean better hours, less travel, staying local and being more available for the girls. *Please, God... Let me get this job.*

But would God answer the prayers of someone like her who found it impossible to forgive others?

Amber threw the cloth into the bin. She missed Ethan. In fact, she ached to see his smile, and the light in his eyes when he said her name. The tenderness on his face when he held her children.

She knew her girls could be a handful. As a single parent, she'd struggled to balance love and discipline with her guilt. What man in his right mind would take on Lucy's and Stella's high spirits and boundless energy?

Ethan, that's who.

She was such an idiot. A prideful, stupid, hardheaded, unreasonable idiot. And she was suddenly sorry, so very sorry—

The bell jangled. Her head snapped up. Uncertainty etched across his handsome face, Ethan stood at the door.

Chapter Eleven

Ethan had stayed away from Amber as long as he could stand it. Until he was overwhelmed by the need to see her. To be with her. To hear her voice.

His hope of bringing Amber and her father together lay in ashes. And if being with Amber meant never mentioning Dwight again, so be it.

Standing in the Mason Jar, Ethan did what he should have done in the first place—prayed. Instead of thinking he knew best; instead of pushing her into a reunion she wasn't ready for.

Help me make this right with her, Father.

A bin loaded with dirty dishes in her arms, she went behind the counter.

He sank onto a stool. "Hey."

Ponytail swishing, she removed an order pad from the back pocket of her jeans. "What would you like?"

He leaned forward, resting his arms on the countertop. "Please forgive me for interfering. For thinking I know what's best for you. I'm sorry, Amber, for not respecting your wishes about Dwight."

Her face crumpled. "Why didn't you tell me about him being with the girls at the dance?"

Ethan ducked his head. "I was afraid you'd be angry."

"I am angry at you, but because you weren't honest with me." Her eyes bored into him. "I've had my fill of dishonest men."

"Things between us were so good. I'd hate to lose our...our friendship."

She looked at him a long, hard moment as he fidgeted on the stool. "So would I. But from here on out there must be only honesty between us. Okay?"

Amber would never understand what had started out as a way to get his grandmother to the beach had evolved into more than he could have ever possibly imagined. Into something he wasn't yet willing to put a name to. But he did know that whatever lay between them was something he'd never experienced before.

Something sweet. Something tender. Something fragile.

Ethan no longer felt the same as he had when he agreed to the deal with his grandmother. But if he told Amber about their bargain now, she'd shut him out. They—he— needed more time. Time for him to regain and solidify her trust in him.

He pushed aside his doubts. Once she graduated, he'd come clean. By then... By then what?

"Ethan?"

He snapped back to the present.

She peered at him. "Is anything wrong? Is there anything else you need to tell me?"

His heart hammered. "Nothing, except you're beautiful." Rising off the stool, he leaned across the counter and planted a quick kiss on her cheek.

She blushed.

"And..."

The vein in the hollow of her throat pulsed a steady beat. "And?" She tilted her head.

"And I wouldn't say no to a piece of pie and coffee."

Her lips quirking, she tucked a strand of hair behind her ear. "You'll ruin your lunch."

Ethan's gaze lingered on the movement of her hand. "I'll take my chances."

Amber Fleming had already ruined more than lunch for him.

Truth was, he was in over his head. And he knew it. So now what did he intend to do about it?

The next week was busy with Amber studying for finals and finishing her last clinicals. She awoke Thursday morning to the sound of rain beating upon the trailer roof. *Ugh.* She buried her face in the pillow.

It would be an ordeal getting the girls in and out of the car. She'd better locate the rain boots Miss IdaLee gave them for Christmas. And pray she'd left the umbrella in the hall closet and not in the car.

"The pink boots awe mine, Stehwaa," Lucy yelped.

"No…" Stella squealed.

There was a thunk. And a shrill cry of juvenile outrage.

Amber threw back the covers. Sometimes two rambunctious little girls felt like legions of children.

With predictions of punishing winds and torrential downpours, the forecasted nor'easter had arrived. And she discovered a notification on her phone informing her that school for the girls was canceled. She would've loved nothing better than to stay home with the twins.

But while school might've closed its doors for the duration, the Mason Jar had not. Ethan would be on twin duty all day. When she pulled into ErmaJean's driveway, he was waiting for them on the porch.

Lucy went into a frenzy of waving. "Efan!"

Stella wagged her fingers. "Ethan!"

Nursing a coffee mug, he looked ridiculously handsome with his tousled hair, T-shirt and his bare feet poking from beneath his jeans. Amber's heart went into overdrive.

As soon as she cut the engine, both girls released the belts buckling them into their booster seats and clambered out of the vehicle.

"Girls. Hold on." She struggled to disengage her seat belt, which appeared to be sticking again. "Let me—" With a whizzing sound, the belt came free and she scrambled after them.

By the time she reached the porch, Ethan had put his mug on the railing and allowed himself to be engulfed by the twins.

Lucy was giving him a blow-by-blow description of everything that had occurred in her life since she saw Ethan last. Yesterday. Tucked up against him, Stella was content to be near him.

Amber sighed. She could relate. She flushed, annoyed with herself.

"Mr. Popularity." She folded her arms. "I'm sorry to unload the girls on you for the whole day."

Ethan smiled that crooked smile of his, which did that fluttery thing to her abdomen. "The weather'll be too bad to work outside, anyway." He looked at her. "The girls, Grandma and I will have a blast together."

Her irritation grew. She told herself it was because she was going to miss out on a day of fun with her children. Which was true. But she was also going to miss sharing the day with him.

And that wasn't acceptable. Not to her peace of mind. He wasn't part of her long-term plan. She wasn't part of his.

She probably shouldn't have come into work today. But she couldn't afford to lose a paycheck. As it turned out, the Mason Jar could have done without her. A few stalwart customers came in for the breakfast special. The sensible ones stayed home.

Through the plate glass window, she watched the weather worsen. For the most part, the streets were deserted. Wind gusts sent the trees on the town square seesawing. A steady deluge of rain battered the roof of the diner.

By eleven, the owner decided to close early. Amber's turn to close the restaurant, the other staff soon departed. She'd just finished mopping the floor when she received a text saying her night class had been canceled. Wonderful. She'd pick up the girls and go home.

The bell jangled.

Without looking up, she set the mop into the bucket of water. "Sorry. I'm afraid we're closed for the—" She went rigid.

Clad in a yellow-striped swift water rescue jacket and hip waders, her father shuffled inside the diner, dripping water on her just-washed floors.

She frowned. "What are you doing here?"

"I came by to see how you were faring."

She planted her hands on her hips. "Five years and two children too late, Dad."

He pushed the hood off his head. "The rain has been coming down hard. Six inches in three hours with more predicted. The rivers and creeks are rising fast. Be careful heading home with the girls. Some roads are already flooded, and your trailer is in a particularly vulnerable area."

"Your belated concern for our well-being is touching."

"I also came to tell you how sorry I am, Amber, for letting you down when you needed me the most."

Her mouth opened. She closed it with a snap.

"I was so lost in my grief." He took a step forward. "It's no excuse, but it was easier to be angry at you for marrying Tony than facing my own pain."

She folded her arms over her chest. "Feel free to gloat. You were right about him. I should've never married him."

Her father shook his head. In the fluorescent lighting, she realized for the first time how silver his hair had become. Grief had a way of aging a person. For an instant, sympathy flickered.

She doused the flame before it had a chance to take hold.

"I would never gloat about Tony hurting you. It was exactly what I feared, but seeing it come to pass gave me no satisfaction."

She swallowed. "I survived. And like you taught me and Matt, what doesn't kill you makes you stronger."

"If I could go back and do that day over again—"

"As I've learned, life doesn't give do-overs."

"Perhaps not, but God gives us second chances." His Adam's apple bobbed. "Two second chances like Lucy and Stella."

Amber drew up. "Don't try seeing them behind my back again, Dad."

He extended his hand. "I'm asking for your forgiveness, Amber. I regret so much. Not the least of which is not knowing those precious children of yours."

She lifted her chin. "Like you once told me, you made your bed hard, and now it's you who has to lie in it."

"I've wished so many times I never said that to you, honey."

Bitterness washed over her. "But you did."

His shoulders slumped. "If there is no forgiveness, love or mercy—" he opened his hands "—what else is left for any of us?"

The words stirred something in her heart. Before she could respond, the handheld radio sticking out of his jacket crackled.

He answered the call. Through the static, Amber surmised the emergency involved a flooded parking lot and people stranded inside the town hall. Signing off, he faced Amber again.

"I've got to go. Another swift water rescue. Fifth one today." His jaw worked. "Don't drive through any standing water. Growing up on the river, you know firsthand the unrelenting force of the current. Maybe you ought to think about staying at ErmaJean's until the storm passes."

"We'll be fine." She motioned to the door. "Don't let me keep you."

"Be careful out there today." His gaze cut to the torrents of rain outside the window. "It's going to get worse before it gets better."

Truer words… Although with Ethan in her life, she was starting to hope the worst was over and that her future was on an upswing.

Her father left the diner. She flicked off the lights and locked the door. Stepping out from underneath the awning, the full force of the squall battered her as she ran for her car.

Driving the short distance to ErmaJean's took longer than usual. The buffeting wind slowed her progress. Pulling into the driveway, she cut the engine and made a dash for the front door.

Pressing the bell, she was surprised when it was Erma-

Jean who answered. The wind caught the door and flung it against the wall with a bang.

"Land sakes, Amber." ErmaJean stepped aside. "Come in. Come in. My, it's nasty out there today."

"Grandma?" Ethan called from the kitchen. "Is everything all right?"

"Right as rain," ErmaJean hollered. She winked at Amber. "So to speak."

Amber was struggling to shut the door when Ethan appeared. Putting his shoulder into it, he wrestled the door closed.

He grinned at her. "Kind of a wet day, huh?"

She rolled her eyes. "As always, the master of the obvious."

From the back of the house, there came a crash.

The three of them flinched.

"Sowee!" Lucy yelled.

"It was an accident," Stella shouted.

The adults exchanged sheepish looks.

"I'm sure they didn't mean to do whatever it was they did," Ethan said.

Amber sighed. "They never do."

"Don't y'all talk about my little sweethearts like that." ErmaJean tilted her chin in the direction of the kitchen. "Be right there, sweet peas." She shuffled down the hall.

All at once, Amber became aware of her drenched clothing. She probably resembled a drowned rat. "I don't want to drip on the carpet so…"

Playfully, he ran his finger across her cheek. "Good thing sugar doesn't melt." The raindrops shimmered on his fingertip. "Or you'd be in trouble." He gave her a lopsided grin.

Butterflies zinged inside her belly. Prickles of awareness danced up and down her arms. Her senses rocketed.

Amber tried for a nonchalance she didn't feel. "So you're saying I'm like sugar?"

"Sugar with a dash of red chili peppers thrown in for good measure." Mischief and something else—something that made her heart palpitate—gleamed in his eyes. "And I think perhaps I've developed a sweet tooth." His teeth flashed white, strong and even.

Unconsciously, or maybe not so unconsciously, she moistened her lips. As if replying to an unspoken invitation, Ethan leaned closer, only inches separating her mouth from his.

Her heart thudded.

"May I?" he murmured.

Always such a gentleman. Even when they were kids, he'd treated her so differently. So tenderly. Her heart cried out for tenderness. Not just from anyone, but from him. Ethan Green, her brother's best friend.

Placing her hands flat on his broad shoulders, she rose on tiptoe. He hadn't moved.

"Amber?" he rasped. "Do you want me to kiss you?" A note of gravelly hesitation laced his voice.

She realized she'd not answered his question.

"Yes, Ethan…" Her breath hitched. "I want you to kiss—"

"Mommy!" Lucy shrilled from the kitchen.

Jerking, she let go of Ethan and came down on her heels, hard. Jolted, he fell face forward into the wall beside her.

"Oh!" She touched his arm.

"Ow!" He touched his face. "Good thing you're a nurse. I have a feeling the training will come in handy over the years."

She smiled. "Let me see." She removed his hand from

his head. "And I'm not a nurse." The skin on his forehead was red but unbroken.

"Not yet."

"Mom-meeeee!"

Amber let her head fall forward where Ethan's shoulder caught it. Laughter rumbled beneath his cotton shirt.

"The troops are calling. You better go before there's a riot." His arms went around her and she seriously considered never moving again. Too quickly, however, he let her go.

"Right." Gulping, she stepped away. "I better get them home before it gets any worse outside."

"Uh, Amber?" He chewed on the inside of his cheek. "I know I said I wasn't going to interfere with your decisions again…" He shuffled his feet.

Amber raised her eyebrow. "But let me guess. You are, anyway?"

He blew out a breath. "It's getting bad out there. The trailer is not in the most ideal location. And your car…" He ran his hand over his head. "Why don't you stay here until the storm passes? Then I could run you all home in the truck."

She pursed her lips. "I appreciate your concern, but all I want to do is go home, put my feet up and watch the rain with the girls."

Amber watched a war wage across his features. But he resisted the urge to butt in, giving her the respect to make her own decisions. For better or for worse.

"Okay," he grunted. "But call me when you get home."

"Will do." She gave him a quick peck on the cheek. Despite the weather, the outlook on her future felt bright with promise.

Immediately, she tempered her optimism. Best not to

get her hopes up. Best to rely on herself. To need only herself. Take life as it came. Day by day.

Ethan caught her arm before she could stage a full-blown retreat to the safety of the kitchen.

"Rain check?" he drawled.

She gave him a sly sideways look. "For what?" And enjoyed his snort of derision.

"You know what, Amber Dawn Fleming."

"You mean you want to kiss me again?" Amber hid her smile. "It'll mean waiting for another rainy day." She started to push a loose tendril of hair behind her ear, but his hand found the strand first.

"Silk," he whispered as he wrapped the lock around his finger. "Some things are worth waiting for." His hand lingered, cupping her ear.

Yes... Some things definitely were.

It was only after loud protests that she herded Lucy and Stella into her car.

"We were having fun with Ethan," Stella grumbled from the back seat.

Amber pulled out of ErmaJean's neighborhood and onto Main Street. The windshield wipers went at break-neck speed in a vain attempt to keep pace with the hammering rain.

"I wish we could stay wif him fowever," Lucy said.

Amber's gaze darted to the rearview mirror. Something treacherously soft within her felt the same. Which wouldn't do. It wouldn't do at all.

"Gigi is out of her cast now." She drove past the shuttered shops and darkened diner. "Which means it won't be long before Ethan will go back to the beach where he really lives."

Although he hadn't said anything about his job or the

beach in a long time. And she was hoping that maybe…
Don't be stupid, Amber.

She didn't need a man. She could stand on her own two feet just fine. Once she graduated, got a job, saved some money and got a better place to live. She was so close to making her dreams come true.

They passed the welcome sign at the town limits. True-love, Where True Love Awaits. Okay, perhaps not so close to making *all* her dreams come true.

"I love Ethan this much."

Glancing in the mirror, Amber watched Stella open her hands.

Not to be outdone, Lucy flung her arms wide. "I wuv Efan dis much."

Stella's eyes narrowed. "I love Ethan the most, Lucy."

"No." Lucy's lip protruded. "I wuv Efan de most, Steh-waa."

The car rattled over the bridge spanning the river.

"Girls, stop arguing. You can both love Ethan the most."

"Mommy?"

The ground on either side of the road was so saturated. With concern, she noted how high the creek had risen.

"Mommy?"

Distracted, she edged around a large puddle in the middle of the road. Fortunately, there was no oncoming traffic. "What, Stella?" She bit her lip. In fact, there was no one else on the winding mountain road.

"Do you love Ethan the most, Mommy?"

Her eyes cut to the mirror. Stella's shrewd little face stared back at her. Amber eased her foot off the accelerator, slowing the car. Did she?

"I—I…"

"Mommy?" Lucy pointed ahead. "What's dat?"

She turned her gaze forward at the same instant the roaring registered. Slamming on the brakes, she watched in sick, fascinated horror as the mountain fell upon them.

The mudslide sucked entire trees into its funnel, snapping them like matchsticks. Boulders tumbled. The surging, flowing stream of mud hit the car broadside.

Lucy screamed.

"Mommy!" Stella shrieked.

"Lucy! Stella!" Amber cried out. "Hang on!"

But to what?

The slide swept the car off the road and into the tributary creek. They were flung like rag dolls against the interior of the car. Rushing along the foaming waterway, everything in front of them was nothing but churning mud and bobbing debris.

Dear God, oh God... Help us.

She grappled with the wheel, but it was no use. She had no control over the vehicle. The raging creek had a mind of its own. Like in a watery pinball machine, the car hurtled downstream, ricocheting off storm-littered obstacles.

Then she spotted it—just ahead—a large boulder in the middle of the creek. The water was pushing them on an inexorable trajectory into a head-on collision. There was no way to avoid it.

Please, please, God. Don't let the rock smash into the back where Lucy and Stella are sitting.

Helpless, Amber gripped the wheel. "Hold on. We're going to crash into that—"

The front passenger side took the full brunt of the blow. Jarred, she screamed. The girls wailed. Metal ground against wet stone. The vehicle fishtailed before coming to a complete, concussive stop. And silence.

For a moment, there was nothing but the sound of the

frothing water bubbling around the car, continuing on its relentless march. Dazed, Amber lifted her head. Her chest heaved.

Disoriented with motion sickness, she put her hand to her head. "Lucy? Stella?" Frantic, her eyes darted to the mirror.

Their gazes locked on to hers.

"Are you all right?"

Their faces unnaturally pale, they nodded.

"Are you bleeding? Does anything hurt?"

Blond hair disheveled, they shook their heads. Only then did she release the breath she hadn't realized she was holding. What had seemed a lifetime since the mountain hit them had in reality only been a few terrifying seconds. Now they were stuck, wedged against the rock in the middle of the normally placid stream.

She became aware of a new, equally menacing, danger. The water was rising. Something freezing cold seeped into the soles of her flats, and she stared in disbelief as murky water rose from the floorboards.

And it kept coming. Powerful. Relentless. Unforgiving.

Biting back a sob, she fought off panic. *Think. Think, Amber.* She'd spent the first twenty years of her life living on the river. Raised by her parents in the rafting business to be a real river rat. She had to stay calm.

Where was her phone? Her hand scrambled for it, but it no longer rested where she'd left it on the console. Probably lying somewhere at her feet where she couldn't get to it.

They had about five minutes—possibly less—before the water would overwhelm the vehicle. First option—they could try to get to the roof and hang on until help arrived.

Amber briefly squeezed her eyes shut. Help would arrive. It had to. Leaving the headlights burning, she turned on the hazard lights to make it easier for rescue personnel to spot them.

Second option—get out and swim for the bank. She gauged the distance. Too far. The girls would never make it. They'd have no chance against the overpowering current.

Why hadn't she allowed Ethan, if not her father, to teach the girls to swim? But she knew why. It was because of her stupid, stupid pride and delusions of self-sufficiency.

Unless completely submerged, the windows should lower. She pressed the button on the door, and the window slowly scrolled down. She hit the lever to release the child safety locks. Next?

She plucked at her seat belt, but it didn't budge. It was stuck. If she couldn't get free, how was she going to help the girls?

Her chin trembled. She was trapped. And time was of the essence. Worst-case scenario—lest she suppose things couldn't get any worse—the car could flip any moment.

She fought to keep the hysteria building inside her chest from escaping into her voice. "Girls, I need you to listen carefully and do exactly what I say."

Tears streaked down their faces.

"Unbuckle your seat belts for me." *Please, God, let them be able.* Sometimes the buckles were tricky for their little fingers.

"I—I can't," Lucy sobbed.

"You can," she encouraged.

With a click, Stella's strap whizzed back, and she was

free. Stella scrambled to help her sister. "Women can do anything, Lucy. Right, Mommy?"

Amber winced. Is that what she'd been teaching her children by example? To depend on themselves and no one else, not even God?

"With God's help, we can do anything, Stella," she corrected. And prayed God would allow her another day, another year, decades, to rectify her parenting errors.

Stella pressed with all her might, and the belt released.

Lucy sprang out of her seat. "Mommy, I can't see my boots in the water."

Amber choked down her fear. "Me, too, sweetheart. Mommy needs you two to do something else. I want you to take off your rain jackets and your boots."

Despite the risks of putting them into the turbulent water, she had to get them out of the car. Footwear would only hamper them. Outer clothing could become caught and entangled in the floating debris, dragging them underneath the water to suffocate and drown.

Amber shuddered. Like what had happened to her mother.

"But my feet will get wet, Mommy," Stella protested.

More than their feet were going to get wet, but she couldn't tell them that. One step at a time. "Girls, try to open the door on Stella's side."

Both girls pushed and pushed. "I can't, Mommy."

"It won't open, Mommy."

Not a complete surprise, but she'd hoped. The water had risen too rapidly, reached a critical threshold. The doors wouldn't open until the water pressure equalized between the outside and the inside of the car. They'd have to wait for the water to fill the car to neck level.

Her neck.

At which point, the girls would have long since

drowned. She had to get them out. No matter what happened to her. Amber's heart hammered. She wasn't sure the girls could climb out the window and hang on to the roof without her help.

"I'm scawed, Mommy," Lucy sobbed.

She felt like sobbing, too. But she couldn't. The girls were already frightened enough.

Images of those she loved flashed before her eyes. The grandmotherly ErmaJean. Her best friend, Callie. Her brother, Matt, stationed in a war zone, who'd believed he was the one in harm's way. And Ethan...

So many regrets. So many dreams unfulfilled.

"We have to pray, Mommy," Stella called from the back seat. "Pray for God to help us."

"That's right, Stella. Lucy." Out of options and at the end of her strength, she leaned against the headrest. "Pray. Pray hard, girls."

Father God... Please save us.

Chapter Twelve

Amber's red taillights had no sooner disappeared down the street before Ethan felt an immense disquiet. And no matter his best efforts to distract himself, the vague feeling of foreboding grew stronger.

His grandmother put away the markers and construction paper the girls had used at the kitchen table. "I wish they hadn't headed up the mountain in these conditions." She switched on the television. Local broadcasters in neon yellow slickers reported from the midst of the storm.

Ethan didn't say anything, just continued to stare out at the pouring rain. Branches littered the yard. The gutter couldn't handle the runoff. Something else to add to his ongoing to-do list.

Anxiety gnawed at his gut. What else could he have done, though? He refused to bully Amber. He'd shared his opinion. Amber had chosen not to accept it. Or his offer of sanctuary from the storm. A metaphor for the larger issues between them.

Uneasiness peppered his thoughts until he could stand it no more.

Ethan removed the truck keys from the peg on the

wall. "I'm going after her. I need to make sure she and the girls got home."

His grandmother looked up from the newscast. "Something isn't right. I have a bad feeling…"

Out in the elements, the wind and rain were merciless, lashing the truck as he pushed through the storm. The truck clattered over the rain-slick bridge, rattling his teeth.

He rounded the curve on the mountain road, and the sight that met his eyes took his breath. He slammed on the brakes. The road was gone.

Piled like Lincoln Logs, massive tree trunks cut him off from the rest of the valley. And if he lived to be a hundred, he'd never forget the horror he felt when he spotted Amber's car wedged broadside against an enormous boulder in the creek. Amber, Lucy and Stella were trapped inside. His girls…

The water already reached the sill of the windows. He sucked in a breath. There was no time to lose. He had to do something. And quick.

He backed the truck as far down the slippery incline as he dared. Thrusting open the door, he was halfway out of the truck when another pickup appeared. It was Jake McAbee and Jonas Stone.

Ethan waved them down. "Amber…" Frantic, he motioned toward the creek.

The men leaped out to assist him. Jonas grabbed a rope from the truck. Over the thunderous rain and fomenting water, Ethan shouted to get Amber's attention.

One of the girls caught sight of him. She said something to Amber in the front seat. The men clambered down the embankment. Ethan didn't understand why Amber didn't get out. Why hadn't she tried to get the girls to the roof?

"I've tied the rope to the hitch on your truck." Jonas gestured. "If we could swim out and get it attached to the steering wheel—"

Just then, Amber's car lurched sideways in the swirling water. Amber and the twins screamed.

Lucy poked her head through the open window. "Efan! Efan!"

"I'm coming," he hollered.

He angled toward the other men. "There's no time to tie it off. Let's wade as far out as we can. Form a chain. Link arms. I'll pass the girls to you one at a time. It's the only way."

Grim-faced, they nodded.

The freezing water hit Ethan like an electric shock. Despite being June, the mountain streams never got very warm. Bracing each other, the guys picked their way across the uneven creek bottom. The fast-flowing current almost knocked them off their feet.

Nearest to the bank, Jonas became the anchor. Then Jake. Finally, in waist-deep water, Ethan stood as close to the rapidly submerging vehicle as the length of their arms allowed.

"Amber," he called.

She turned her head toward the open window. Tears glistened on her pale, beautiful cheeks. Her face wore a pinched expression. He didn't like the resigned look in her shadowed eyes.

"Take the girls," she rasped. "Get them out. Save my babies, Ethan."

"I'm getting all of you out." He lifted his chin. "You take one. I'll take the other. Jake and Jonas will make sure we don't lose our footing."

She shook her head. The wet, bedraggled strands of

water-darkened hair clung to her cheekbones. "You don't understand. I can't get out. My seat belt is stuck."

He clenched his jaw. "There's a box cutter in my glove compartment. I'll get it, and cut you out."

"There's no time, Ethan. Please." Her gaze clouded. "It doesn't matter about me. Just save Lucy and Stella."

"It does matter about you." He gritted his teeth. "I won't leave you."

"Stella, climb out onto the window and jump as far as you can. Ethan will catch you." Those beautiful blue eyes of hers filled with tears. "Won't you, Ethan?"

"Mommy…" Stella's teeth chattered with the first signs of hypothermia.

"I love you, Stella. You must be brave, honey. Quickly now for your sister's sake. It's Lucy's turn next."

Scrunching her face, his stoic, brave little Stella did as her mother bade her. Hanging on to the car frame, she clambered out.

"Come to me, Stella Bella," he coached.

Biting her lower lip—so like her mother his heart faltered—Stella took a deep breath and launched herself at his outstretched arms. She gasped as the water hit her bare legs but he caught her and she didn't go under.

She wrapped her arms in a stranglehold around his neck. He tried to pass her to Jake, but she didn't let go.

"Let Jake take you to the truck, sweetheart. You like riding in my truck, don't you?" He kissed the top of her head. "I have to help Lucy."

"And Mommy."

Anguish clawed at his insides. "And Mommy, too." With a determined wrench, he thrust Stella into Jake's arms.

Dwight's SUV screeched to a standstill. He threw

himself out, sliding down the embankment. "Amber!" he yelled.

Stark fear ravaged his rugged features. He snagged the rope Jonas had tied to Ethan's hitch and knotted it around his waist. "I'm coming, Amber!"

But he wouldn't be in time. Her gaze locked on to Ethan's. They both knew Dwight wouldn't be in time.

"Callie. ErmaJean. My dad…" Her voice quavered. Swallowing, she gave Ethan a small smile. "You will all look after Lucy and Stella, won't you?"

Something shattered inside his heart.

"Lucy?" Ethan called. He wouldn't give up. If they hurried…

But Lucy clung to her mother's seat. "No, Efan. I scawed."

Reaching backward, Amber pried Lucy's hands from around the headrest. "You must go. Now." Twisting in the seat, she shoved her daughter toward the opening.

"Ow, Mommy," Lucy cried. "No…"

"I love you, Lucy." She kept pushing Lucy over the sill. "I love you, Stella!" she yelled.

Lucy flung herself at him. Lunging, Ethan caught her. But Jonas lost his grip on Ethan's arm. Ethan and Lucy went under. Never for an instant letting go of Lucy, he kicked against the bottom. Clasping her tight against his chest, they surged upward, sputtering.

Jonas snagged hold of Ethan's shirt, and the cowboy fought a desperate battle to keep them from being sucked downstream. Then with Lucy between them, he and Jonas dragged themselves onto the shoreline.

Dwight had thrown himself into the maelstrom. The former collegiate swimmer battled the current. His still-powerful arms plowed through the water in a valiant attempt to reach his daughter.

Ethan would have gone in after him, but with a hand on his shoulder, Jonas stopped him. "You can't help him. You're exhausted. You'd only drown yourself."

Jake handed Stella into his arms alongside Lucy. "Amber would want you to be here for her girls."

His legs quivering like a jellyfish, Ethan sank onto the sand. Wet and shivering, he turned the girls' faces into his chest to keep them from seeing what would surely happen next. Helpless to do anything else.

Except watch their mother drown.

It was with a surreal detachment Amber watched her father fight with everything in his stubborn, never-quit nature to reach her. The same stubborn nature she'd inherited from him, which had helped her survive the last five long years.

But he was no match against the force of the current. He hadn't been able to save her mother. Now, though, she understood how much he'd tried. And how broken it had left him. Left them both.

The cold water seemed to have seeped into the very marrow of her bones. Listless, she closed her eyes. Truth be told, she was so tired of fighting.

Fighting life. Fighting herself. Fighting God.

She'd made so many mistakes. The least of which was marrying Tony. *Please forgive me, God.*

Water lapped at her chin.

Is this what it had felt like for her mother that day on the river? Had she fought to the bitter end not to leave her family? Or had she simply let go and drifted. Far beyond the pain and sadness. The—

"Amber!"

Her eyes snapped open. Hanging on to the side of the car, her father sucked in oxygen, his chest heaving.

"D-Daddy?" She swallowed a mouthful of water. She choked, coughing.

"Tilt your head back as far as you can. Keep your face out of the water." One arm hooked over the open window, he removed a retractable utility knife from his pocket. "I won't lose you, too." Leaning in, with his arms underwater, he sawed at the seat belt strapping her in place.

"Daddy…" she whispered. "It's okay."

"It will be. Just you see." Jaw clenched, he sliced at the belt. "Lucy and Stella will not lose their mother the way you lost yours."

"Dad." She touched his arm. "It wasn't your fault what happened to Mom. I know that now."

The pastor's words floated across her consciousness. In the blink of an eye, everything had changed. *Forgive often*, he'd said. *Love with all your heart.* She would never have that chance again.

"What happened between us was as much my fault as yours, Dad."

His face set, her father continued to lacerate the fraying belt.

"I forgive you for what you said. Please forgive me for shutting you out of my life."

A lone tear tracked across his cheek. "I forgive you. I love you, Amber." He gave the fabric a final, vicious tug. It snapped, and she was free.

With an almost superhuman strength born of adrenaline and a parent's worst nightmare, he wrested her from the sinking vehicle. Once she was out of the car and in the water with him, he wrapped his arms around her.

"Pull!" he shouted to the men on shore.

There was a tug on the rope wrapped around her father's waist. Hand over hand, the men reeled them in toward the bank. Her feet scraped bottom. *Thank You, God. Thank You.*

She found herself enfolded in the fiercely protective arms of Ethan. And she wondered if that wasn't exactly where she'd belonged from the beginning. For once, her what-if fears silenced.

Chapter Thirteen

The storm blew out as quickly as it had blown in, but Ethan felt the near-drowning had probably taken at least five years off his life.

Dwight insisted on everyone getting checked out by emergency medical personnel. Thankfully, bruises and scrapes were the worst of it for all of them. Afterward, Amber invited her dad to the trailer, and she properly introduced their grandfather to Lucy and Stella.

Pulling Ethan and her mother to the side, Lucy whispered, "Is he one of the good daddies?"

Amber glanced at her father playing Chutes and Ladders on the coffee table with Stella. "Yes, Lucy." Amber's eyes pricked with tears. "He is."

She spent the next week getting reacquainted with her father. There were a lot of tears, but also hugs and laughter, too.

Cleanup commenced in putting Truelove back to rights. The DOT reopened the road to traffic. With her car a total loss, Dwight insisted she allow him to find her another, more reliable vehicle.

"Only a loan," Amber—being Amber—reluctantly agreed. "I'll pay you back. Every cent, Dad."

The town paper made much over the four men, much to their mutual embarrassment. The day of the storm, despite Amber's protests, Dwight had left the town hall determined to check on his daughter. Jake and Jonas had been helping the pastor secure the church and were returning to their respective homes when they ran across the accident.

A coincidence? Ethan thought not. Definitely a God thing.

As for his impending departure? There was so much he needed to do: starting with putting Grandma's house on the market. Contact a moving company. Put a deposit on one of the cottages. Not the least of which, he needed to call to his buddy in Wilmington at the boat shop. But the days ticked by without him getting around to any of it.

Because he'd had to finish the two end tables a customer had ordered. Then he spent some extra time with his girls—just to reassure his heart they were truly safe. And, of course, Grandma required a great deal of supervision. Especially when she and the matchmakers got together.

Ethan also got to know Jake and Jonas better. Surrounded by Truelove women, he'd missed the camaraderie of men. They were great guys.

Something had shifted in his relationship with Amber. The following weekend, Jonas's mother, Deirdre, held a celebratory dinner at the Fielding-Stone ranch for all the families involved in the rescue.

After eating, Jonas's son, Hunter, Maisie and the twins were excused to play. The adults helped Deirdre clear the table.

"I knew my Jake was a hero." Rising on tiptoe, Callie planted a kiss on Jake's beard-stubbled jaw. "And now everyone else knows, too." He reddened.

Ethan chuckled. Jake was a pretty good guy, even if he was ex-army.

Amber nudged Jonas with her hip as she passed by, her hands full of plates. "I owe you free nursing care for life."

"The dude ranch could always use a part-time nurse on call." Jonas smiled. "I reserve the right to take you up on that."

And Amber smiled back.

Scowling into his empty tea glass, Ethan drifted out the French doors and onto the veranda. She could smile at anyone she chose. What was it to him?

He leaned against the wooden railing, staring at the blue-green mountain vista. Was he jealous? Of Amber and Jonas? His heart did a stutter step against his rib cage.

And before he had time to digest that unsettling revelation, she followed him outside. "Hey." She touched his back.

He straightened. "Hey yourself."

She pointed at his forehead. "How's your head?"

His brow furrowed. "My head?"

"The day of the storm. You fell into the wall." She smiled. "Therefore, you get first dibs on my nursing skills."

Something tight eased in his chest.

"That's right." He threw her a lazy smile. "And come to think of it, I could use a little nursing TLC right now." He cut his eyes at her. "You might be the only one in the whole world who can make me feel better."

"Oh, really? In the whole world?" She raised her eyebrow. "Where does it hurt?"

He tapped his forehead. "Here."

She placed her palm against his skin. "You don't have a fever."

"Oh, but I do." He cocked his head. "I truly do. Scout's honor."

She rolled her eyes. "You were never a Boy Scout."

"What if you were to kiss it?" He bit his lip to keep from laughing. "I'm pretty sure it would feel better."

She gave him a quick kiss on his forehead. "How's that?"

"Better." He moved his finger to his cheek. "But then there's this spot here."

"That hurts, too? My, my," she tsk-tsked. "You're in kind of bad shape for such a young guy."

Setting the tea glass on the railing, he placed his hand over his heart. "What can I say? Thanks to the Fleming women, Truelove has proven only slightly less dangerous than my entire military career."

"Put that way, it becomes my patriotic duty to assist you." She pressed her lips against his cheekbone. "There." She stepped away. "All better."

Taking hold of her forearms, he walked her backward until her spine pressed against the wooden post. Then he captured her lips with his mouth. He ran his fingers through her hair. She wasn't like the other women he'd known. More important, he wasn't the same man he'd once been.

Ethan pulled back. Amber's eyes had darkened to an inky blue. Her reaction left him with a profound sense of protectiveness. Of responsibility.

He kept his arms around her, not letting her drift far. "We better cool it before Grandma catches us." He laughed. "Or Lucy."

Amber's beautiful lips curved. "And Stella."

"Next week this time, you'll be walking across a stage."

Gaze lowered, she clutched the front of his shirt. "I really like you, Ethan Todd Green."

He touched his finger to her chin, tilting her chin upward. He didn't like not being able to see her stunning eyes—a window to her soul. "And I really, really like you, Amber Dawn Fleming."

Amber's lips twitched. "Sounds like what we have here, folks, is a mutual admiration society."

He swallowed. He was unsure of what would follow her nursing school graduation. Uncertain where he and Grandma would be. Unable to voice his concerns.

Because, suddenly, he was very much afraid his feelings for Amber had gone far, far beyond anything remotely resembling mere admiration.

Standing on the stage with the other nursing candidates for the pinning ceremony at the community college, Amber thought this might be the happiest day of her life.

The day the twins were born had been a bittersweet mix of happiness and fear for the future. Four years ago, she'd been alone in the Labor and Delivery room in Asheville. But she'd been determined to take care of the precious gifts God had placed in her arms. To be worthy of her children.

On that day, her journey truly began. No longer thinking of herself, she put their welfare first. It had been a humbling, at times painful, path that brought her home to Truelove.

Arriving divorced and alone with twin baby girls to raise. Taking any job she could get. Sacrificing sleep and time with them to pursue this degree program.

Striving to better herself and their situation. Five semesters later, after 756 hours of classwork and clinicals, she was ready to graduate.

Fifteen graduates in this year's accelerated Bachelor of Nursing program sat in two rows across the stage. The audience was filled with friends, family and well-wishers. Ensconced between Ethan and ErmaJean, Lucy waved energetically from her seat. With a shy smile, Stella wriggled her fingers at her mother.

Sitting beside Callie, Amber's father gave her a thumbs-up. Miss GeorgeAnne and Miss IdaLee were also in attendance. Everyone wore their Sunday best dresses, suits and ties.

Perched on the edge of her seat, Amber smoothed the floral print dress over her knees. A graduation present from the matchmakers.

The Dean of Nursing called the nursing candidates forward, one by one, to present their diploma. A friend or family members joined them onstage to present a rose and do the pinning.

Awaiting her turn, she basked in the long-anticipated moment. For once, everything in her life was coming together. Everyone she loved was within sight. Her dreams were finally coming true.

Did those dreams include Ethan? Her heart skipped a beat. Yes, they did.

He'd made a new life for himself in Truelove. Successfully restarted his grandfather's business. Made new friends. Carved out a place for himself not only in the town, but in their hearts. Lucy's. Stella's.

And hers?

There was so much to look forward to. So much ahead for them. She could hardly wait for this new season in her life to unfold.

God had blessed her so much by bringing Ethan into their lives. She wasn't sure yet what he felt for her.

Friendship for sure. He'd proven he loved her children. Maybe one day he'd fall in love with her, too.

Might she fall in love with him one day? Perhaps today? On this day of new beginnings, dare she put a name to the feelings he inspired within her?

"Amber Dawn Fleming…"

Rising, she went forward to the podium. Holding Lucy's and Stella's hands, Ethan led the girls onto the stage.

Stella took the pin from the dean, and carefully, as if it were made of spun glass, handed off the pin to Ethan. Leaning to pin it to Amber's collar, his pine-scented cologne wafted across her nostrils. Butterflies danced in her belly.

"I'm so proud of you," he whispered.

For an instant, she became lost in his gaze until Lucy thrust a single stemmed red rose into her hand.

Applause broke out, and the moment passed as the next candidate's name was called. Ethan helped the girls off the stage, and they resumed their seats in the auditorium. He threw Amber that ridiculously knee-buckling smile of his. She sat down again, grateful for the sturdiness of the chair.

Later, the dean gave an inspiring speech about service to others. Amber was glad it was brief as the twins would have found it difficult to sit still for much longer. Once the ceremony concluded, the guests were invited to enjoy a reception in the atrium.

She lingered in the auditorium for a few minutes, thanking her professors for their part in helping her succeed. She took a few selfies with fellow classmates. They wished each other well. Promised to stay in touch.

Floating into the reception, the girls rushed forward and hugged her. Ethan raised a glass of lemonade to her in a silent toast. She was engulfed by the congratulations of friends and family.

Callie and Amber's father helped the girls go around the buffet table and load their plates. Dwight was sweet with them, getting into grandpa mode. She was so thankful he was in their lives.

She gazed around the crowded reception hall. She'd done it. It hadn't been easy. She could have never done this alone—without God, ErmaJean, her children's patience and Ethan. Perhaps that had been the lesson she needed to learn.

"I'll be right back." She patted Ethan's shoulder. "I left something in the car."

"Let me get it for you. Stay here and enjoy your moment."

"That's okay. I'll get it. I have a thank-you gift for your grandmother."

She scanned the room, but didn't spot ErmaJean. Perhaps she was in the ladies' room. If she hurried... "Maybe while I dash out, you could make sure Little Miss Mischief and Little Miss Mayhem don't do anything ill-advised."

His lips quirked. "Like what?"

"I don't know... Like overturn the food table. Start a riot." She threw out her hands. "Burn down the building."

He cocked his head. "Mischief and mayhem? You must have those wonderful girls confused with someone else's twins."

She rolled her eyes.

"Have I told you how beautiful you look today, Amber?"

She blushed. Surrounded by the people she loved, she felt more than beautiful today. She felt radiant.

Brushing against her arm, he leaned closer. "Hurry back so I can rectify my error, okay?"

Her pulse raced. "Okay," she rasped.

Across the reception area, her father laughed at something Lucy said. Her heart full, Amber drifted out the glass doors. Taking a shortcut to the parking lot, she rounded the corner of the building only to hear GeorgeAnne's voice at the other end of the terrace.

Amber rocketed to a stop beside a large holly bush. Much as she loved the old lady, if GeorgeAnne got hold of her she'd never make it to the car. Perhaps she should retrace her steps and head out the front instead. Then the details of the unseen conversation penetrated her consciousness.

"Ethan's fulfilled his part of the bargain, ErmaJean. What is to stop him from insisting you honor your end of the deal?"

What deal was GeorgeAnne talking about? Amber poked her head around the bush.

"After I broke my leg and Ethan demanded I return with him to the coast, I had to do something." Apparently, Ethan's grandmother wasn't in the ladies' room. "And if it meant getting Amber to graduation, it was a risk I was willing to take."

"GeorgeAnne and I would miss you terribly if you move to Wilmington." IdaLee frowned. "And I think you would be unhappy there, too. This is your home, ErmaJean."

"But all's well that ends well." ErmaJean smirked. "Exactly as I'd hoped. As a matter of fact…"

Heading down the stone steps, the three women moved out of earshot.

Amber's heart pounded. What bargain had Ethan

made with his grandmother? And what did any of it have to do with her graduation?

It almost sounded like… No. She shook her head. It couldn't be what she suspected. Ethan wouldn't use her and the twins to leverage his grandmother into moving away from Truelove. Would he?

Doing an about-face, she returned to the reception hall and found Ethan chatting with Callie.

His face lit. "That was quick."

She clenched her hands. "We need to talk."

His brow creased. "What's wrong?"

"Now, Ethan," she growled.

He and Callie exchanged glances.

Callie backed away. "Why don't I go check on the girls?"

He touched Amber's sleeve.

She drew up. "I think it would be better if we went outside so we can have this conversation in private."

His gaze clouded. "If that's what you want." He followed her onto the terrace.

What she wanted? She ground her teeth. What she'd wanted was him. And a new life with the girls. Maybe she was reading more into the matchmakers' remarks than she should.

God, please let me be wrong.

She made it no farther than the last time. At the holly bush, she rounded on him. "Is it true you made a deal with your grandmother that in exchange for twin-sitting until I graduated, ErmaJean would move to Wilmington with you?"

He was silent. Her stomach knotted. She could see in his eyes, her worst fears were true. He hadn't denied her accusations. And her heart shattered into a million pieces.

"When ErmaJean was released from the hospital and

neither of you said anything more about her relocating, I believed you'd dropped the issue. Obviously, I was mistaken." Her chest heaved. "About a lot of things."

"Amber—"

"Did you or did you not practically blackmail your grandmother into this arrangement?"

Ethan swallowed. "It wasn't like—"

"Have you been pretending all along to care about my children?"

Ethan's eyes widened. "What? No! I do care about them. I love Lucy and Stella."

And they loved him. This day was turning into her worst nightmare.

"Was anything you said to me for real? Or was I just a convenient way to pass the time in boring, old Truelove?"

She'd fallen for his charm hook, line and sinker. Had she learned nothing from the disaster of her marriage to Tony? All her doubts and feelings of inadequacy came roaring back.

"If you'll let me explain…" He took hold of her arm.

She snatched herself free. "Congratulations. I've graduated and now you can force your grandmother to move to Wilmington."

"Don't do this, Amber." He opened his hands. "You have your degree. Neither of us is tied here any longer. There are so many possibilities. We can make this work. It doesn't have to be this way."

Her laugh was without mirth. "Who are you kidding? We were always going to end up right where we are." She made a sweeping gesture. "Me with the twins. And having done your good deed for the decade, you can be off on your merry way again."

Despite her best efforts, her eyes welled. "You've been quite the Good Samaritan. Loving the poor little fatherless girls. This just proves we could never be happy together."

She'd been so easy to deceive. Only because she'd so desperately wanted it to be true—having Ethan in her life. For a moment, she thought she detected movement in the bushes.

"That's not how I felt," he grunted. "That's not how I feel."

"How do you feel, Ethan? About me? About taking on fatherhood?"

Ethan raked his hand over his hair. "I—I—"

"That's what I thought. I told you from the beginning—we're a package deal, me and the girls."

"I can't talk to you when you're like this." His mouth flattened. "When you've calmed down, we can—"

"Don't you *dare* tell me to calm down." She stiffened. "I let myself believe you were different. But you're just like Tony."

He sucked in a breath. "I'm nothing like Tony. How dare you compare me to their no-good dad." He scrubbed his face. "I'm going to leave now before we say things that can't be taken back."

"Run away. After all, that's what you do best. Just like Tony." She jutted her jaw. "Worse than that, you're just like your father."

Anger and hurt blazed from his eyes.

She tossed her hair over her shoulder. "It's amazing, isn't it? One misguided decision can haunt the rest of your life." She lifted her chin. "Well, you're about to discover that truth for yourself. Enjoy the beach, Ethan."

"Have your pride, Amber." His face hardened. "But I think you'll find it a cold comfort. Let me know when you want to talk."

"I don't want to talk to you, Ethan. In fact, don't let

us keep you from your wonderful life. I don't ever want to see you again."

Suddenly, her father came onto the terrace. "Sorry to interrupt. Are the girls out here with you and Ethan?"

"I haven't seen them." Her lip curled. "And the girls won't be seeing so much of him from now on. Actually, none of us will. Isn't that right, Ethan?"

Amber's father looked between them. "What's wrong, honey?"

"Nothing." Her eyes bored into Ethan's. "Everything's exactly as it was always meant to be."

Ethan's face fell, and then almost as quickly, anger licked the broad planes of his features. Turning on his heel, he stalked up the stone steps and disappeared into the atrium. She started to shake.

Her father touched her sleeve. "Amber, sweetheart."

If she didn't get out of here this minute, she was going to fall apart.

"Dad…" She inhaled sharply. "Would you mind spending the rest of the day with Lucy and Stella? I'd really like some alone time, if that's all right with you."

Her father's brow furrowed. "Of course, honey. I love spending time with them, but what's—"

"I need to go, Dad. Please thank everyone for me."

She staggered toward the parking lot. Nothing had gone as she'd hoped today. Perhaps losing Ethan meant nothing ever would.

Chapter Fourteen

The next morning at the house, Ethan threw a handful of shirts into his duffel bag.

"So that's it, then?" Grandma folded her arms. "You're going to pack up and leave?"

"Amber won't let me explain." Yanking out a drawer from the bureau, he dumped his socks on top of the shirts. "She won't listen."

Last night, his grandmother had called Amber in an attempt to mitigate the blame for coming up with the scheme in the first place. To no avail.

"And if she did listen?" Grandma sank onto the mattress. "What would you tell her, Ethan?"

"The truth." He rammed the drawer back into the bureau. "That this whole thing began as a way to get you to move closer to me and also make sure Amber finished school."

"Don't know that I'd start there." His grandmother shook her head. "Amber hates being the object of pity."

"It wasn't pity, Grandma. We were both invested in her success. Success meant her finishing school. And after you broke your leg, she couldn't do that without someone stepping in to take care of the girls. Sure, I was reluctant about twin-sitting at first, but then..." He scraped his hand over his face.

"Then?"

He sighed. "Then Lucy and Stella staked a claim to my heart. I love spending time with them. I love *them*."

"Of course you do." Grandma nodded. "The real question is, what are you going to do about it?"

"There's nothing I can do to convince Amber things are not as she imagines." He glared. "Why can't she see that people care about her and the girls? Why must she shut everyone out?"

"She's been hurt, badly, and has lost her ability to trust anyone but herself."

"I'd thought—hoped—she was beginning to trust me. See that I wasn't like her ex-husband. But now...? I have no one to blame but myself. I should've trusted her and been honest with her." He threw up his hands. "She wants me out of the girls' lives. Out of her life."

His grandmother gazed at him over the top of her reading glasses. "And since when have you ever done anything anyone told you to do? You need to tell Amber how you feel."

"I did, Grandma."

"Not just about her girls, but about her, too."

His chest tightened. Amber had asked him how he felt, and he'd come up empty, unable—unwilling?—to articulate his feelings. "I don't know what you mean. Amber is Matt's sister. A friend."

"A friend?" Grandma snorted. "I've seen the way you look at her. That excuse is wearing thin."

"So she's a very good friend." He set his jaw. "Amber and the girls have become dear to me."

Grandma raised her eyes to the ceiling. "This is what I deal with, Lord." Her mouth pursed. "The problem is that neither of you can be honest about how you feel for each other. You're in love with Amber. And I strongly believe she is in love with you."

His mouth fell open. "That's not true."

She cocked her head. "Which part? About her loving you, or you loving her?"

"Either. Both. Neither." He growled. "All of it. That wasn't the deal, Grandma. This was supposed to be a temporary arrangement."

She lifted her chin. "So you're still determined to leave Truelove? You'll be okay never seeing Amber or the girls again?"

"I…"

Ethan swallowed. Leaving Truelove forever had been his plan. A plan that didn't seem as appealing now for a multitude of reasons. He'd not counted on his mountain hometown growing on him as it had. Nor two adorable blonde four-year-olds. But there was their mother to consider.

As if he could seriously forget her. He couldn't go a quarter of an hour without Amber consuming his thoughts. And the idea of never seeing them again? Not being able to watch the girls grow up. Not being a part of their lives; it tore him up inside in a way he'd not anticipated.

Left him feeling hollow in a way he'd sworn never to feel again—not after his dad abandoned them. Maybe he did have father issues.

For the first time in years, he'd been happy. Really happy. Grandma, the girls and Amber had filled his life with laughter and a sense of rightness. But now?

He dropped his chin. "If I leave within the hour, I'll reach Wilmington before dark."

"So you're still determined to leave?"

"What else can I do? There is nothing here for me. No future with her."

"She's hurt and confused right now—"

"Join the club," he muttered.

"What if you gave her time to get used to the idea?"

The what-ifs were eating him alive.

"She's made her feelings clear regarding my continued presence in their lives. I have to respect her wishes." He ran his hand over his head. "But don't worry. You don't have to go with me."

His grandmother's eyes narrowed. "But what about our agreement?"

"You've got lots of friends in Truelove. A great support network. And the matchmakers. Your whole life is here. There's no reason for you to leave."

Grandma looked at him. "Except for you."

Ethan shrugged. "We'll call. Text. You can visit."

His grandmother's shoulders sagged. "Where's your support network, Ethan?"

Ethan swallowed. "I'll get by. I always do."

"You mean you'll exist." His grandmother's chin wobbled. "And not happily."

But that was the way of things. He'd learned that lesson as a boy. Nothing lasted forever. Certainly not happiness.

He blew out a breath. "I guess I needed you more than you ever needed me. Some things never change, huh?"

"Ethan…" She reached for him, but he moved away.

"I need to get on the road pretty soon."

She rose. "I'll go with you, sweetheart."

"No… I won't allow you to sacrifice your life for me." He grimaced. "Again."

She blocked his escape. "You were never a sacrifice, honey. You were a gift to your granddad and me."

A hollow feeling resided where once his heart dwelled. "I was wrong about you leaving Truelove, Grandma."

She lifted her chin. "A change would be good for both of us. Sand between my toes. Ocean waves. Sea breezes."

"You're part of Amber's support network. Lucy's and Stella's, too. I won't take you away from them."

"Amber has her father now. Dwight and the girls will spend a lot of time together. She has good friends like Callie and the Stones. But you, sweetheart…" Grandma touched her worn palm to his face. "What do you have?"

He had nothing without Amber and the girls. His stomach lurched. He wanted nothing but Amber and the girls.

"I love you for offering to come with me, Grandma." He kissed her cheek. She smelled of everything good from his childhood—like lavender and snickerdoodle cookies. "But this is your home. And when you find a forever home, you don't ever let it go."

For a time, he'd begun to imagine Truelove might be his home. But like so many things in his life, it was not to be.

"I want you to find your forever home, too, Ethan."

"Maybe I will." His tone became wistful. "Someday. Maybe sand, sea breezes and ocean waves were always meant to be my future. Perhaps I'll find it there, but…" He swallowed. "Just not here."

"I can't tell you how sorry I am this didn't work out for you. The matchmakers and I had so hoped…" Biting her lip, she looked away.

As he'd suspected, a well-meaning but a doomed-to-failure conspiracy to throw him and Amber together.

"Not all of us get a happily-ever-after, Grandma." He sighed. "But I hope Amber gets hers. She deserves someone wonderful."

"*You're* wonderful, Ethan."

He shook his head. "And more than anything, I pray the girls get their forever daddy." His voice choked. "It just wasn't ever supposed to be me, I guess."

Ethan needed to get out of here before he lost it in front of his grandmother. He'd stopped crying the day his dad walked out. What was the point? Tears were a wasted action.

In his pocket, his cell phone buzzed. He almost didn't answer it, in no mood to talk to anyone. But force of habit prevailed, and he dug the phone out of his jeans.

He glanced at the screen. "It's—" His eyes darting to his grandmother, he answered it. "Amber?"

"Are Lucy and Stella with you?" Her words came out in a rush. "With Miss ErmaJean? Have you seen—"

"Wait, wait. Slow down." His heart pounded. "I don't understand what you're saying. What's wrong?"

"Lucy and Stella, they're gone. They've run away." Panic laced her voice. "I've searched everywhere. I don't know what to do."

"How do you know they've run away?" His grip tightened on the phone. "If someone has taken the girls, we need to call—"

"I've called the police, and they're out looking. So is my dad. The girls left a note." She swallowed a sob. "But you're right. Someone could've... Anything could happen to them."

His heart slammed against his rib cage. "Where are you, Amber?"

"I—I'm at the trailer. This is all my fault, Ethan. If I'd been a better mother—" She sobbed into the phone.

"Stay where you are. I'm coming," he spoke into the receiver. "I'll have Grandma alert the matchmakers. We'll find them, Amber. They can't have gone far. It's going to be okay."

His grandmother grabbed his sleeve. "What's happened?" Her blue eyes clouded with fear.

Ethan clicked off and scrubbed his hand over his face. The twins were so little. And so vulnerable. "Lucy and Stella have run away."

Grandma put her hand to her throat. "Amber must be going crazy with worry."

"And blaming herself."

His grandmother's mouth trembled. "It's what she does when something goes wrong. Whereas you…" She bit her lip.

"Whereas I run." He squared his shoulders. "But not this time, Grandma."

When Ethan's truck pulled into her driveway, Amber quickly locked the trailer door and clambered into the passenger seat beside him.

His gaze raked over her tear-streaked features. "Tell me what happened, Amber. When did you last see the girls?"

Unable to keep her hands still, she swept her hair behind her head into an untidy bun. "We need to go look for them."

"Take a breath. Let's think through this first. Did something happen this morning?"

"Lucy and Stella were so quiet when Dad brought them home after the reception yesterday. Too quiet." Her mouth trembled. "I think they must've overheard us arguing on the terrace. And when you left…"

He'd stormed out of the reception—not his proudest moment.

She took a breath. "Last night, they looked so sad. I

should've talked to them at breakfast, but I was upset."
Her blue eyes blazed with anguish. "I thought seeing
me cry would be worse. So I went into my bedroom and
shut the door."

His heart jackknifed. Amber had been crying. Because of him.

"I was only gone for ten minutes, but by the time I
dried my eyes and came out, they were gone."

She reached into her pocket and withdrew a scrap of
paper torn from a pre-K writing tablet. The kind with a
dashed red line positioned between two blue bold, solid
placement lines.

He scanned the note, written in crayon with Stella's
strong, if messy, penmanship.

MOMMY AND ETHAN,
BE HAPPY.
LUV,
LUCY AND STELLA

His mouth tightened. "Did they take anything with
them?"

"Their school backpacks are missing. The book you
gave them." She swiped at her eyes. "And, of all things,
a container of leftovers from the fridge."

"What leftovers?"

"It doesn't make sense. They don't even like vegetables. None of this makes any sense. If anything happens
to them, Ethan…" Her voice broke.

He took her in his arms. "Don't think like that."

She sobbed into his shirt. "Why does everyone leave
me? My mother. Tony. My dad."

If she'd only given him a chance, he would've never
left her. Or those girls of hers he loved more than life it-

self. But he couldn't say those things to her. She wanted no future with him. He had only himself to blame.

Ethan figured she'd only called him out of sheer desperation.

His arms tightened around her. "We'll pray for God to show us where to find them, Amber. And pray He will protect them until we can get to them."

"You want to pray? With me?" Tears streaking her face, she lifted her head. "You really have changed, haven't you?"

"With God all things are possible." He cradled her face in his hands. "And I'm choosing to believe God will help us to find the girls. Don't lose faith, Amber. God is here with you." His voice thickened. "And so am I."

She'd called him, hadn't she? That had to mean something. That on some level she still trusted him, if only a little.

Her eyes pooled. "Thank you, Ethan. After what happened yesterday…"

"The only thing that matters is finding Lucy and Stella." He tightened his jaw. "I won't rest until the girls are safely home in your arms. Where they belong."

Amber had felt so safe and right in his arms.

He'd been so sweet and tender not only with her, but with her girls, too. Maybe she'd overreacted about his and ErmaJean's arrangement. Stumbling over her pride yet again. Had she learned nothing from the estrangement with her father?

But she couldn't think about that now. She had to find her girls before it was too late.

"God, please don't let us be too late," she whispered.

Ethan's strong hands gripped the wheel, but he closed

his eyes. "Yes, Lord," he rasped. "Show us without delay where to turn first."

Her heart quivered at the intensity and raw faith etched across his handsome features. He wasn't the same reckless boy she'd known. He was a man who devotedly loved her children. And his God.

Ethan opened his eyes. There was a peace in his gaze. "I have an idea of where they might have gone. Vegetables, you said? What book?"

She shrugged. "Corn. Peas. The duckling book."

"They've gone to the pond, Amber." Some of the tension left his face. "To see the ducks."

Her brow puckered. "But that's too far for them to have wandered alone. If someone saw them walking on the road and picked them up…"

Ethan took hold of her hand, lacing his fingers in hers. "Suppose they didn't take the road?"

"You mean through the woods?"

He nodded. "As the crow flies, not that far from the trailer." He made a face. "And I'm the one who showed them the deer trail. I'm sorry."

She squeezed his hand. "You would never intentionally put them in harm's way, Ethan. I know that."

He studied her face. "Nor you, either, Amber." Breaking eye contact, he ran his hand over his head. "The road will get us there quicker." He cranked the engine and set the truck in motion. "Text your dad. Let him know where we're headed."

The pitted driveway jostled her.

She fell against him. "Sorry." Flicking him an embarrassed glance, she scooted back to her side of the vehicle and got out her phone.

A muscle jumped in his cheek. But he kept his gaze trained on the gravel drive, not looking at her.

He nosed the truck out onto the paved secondary road. Minutes later, he veered onto the rough farm track. There were more bumps as the truck lurched past the split-log fencing and the hay-filled meadow.

When they rounded a clump of trees, she sat forward on the seat, willing the truck to go faster. She knotted her hands.

Please, let them be here, God. Let them be safe.

"There!" He pointed to the windshield.

Her heart thumped. Their blond hair glimmering in the sunshine, the twins tossed handfuls of corn at the ducks.

At the sound of the vehicle, both girls looked up and froze. He slowed, but throwing open the door, she clambered out of the truck before he could bring it to a standstill.

She ran toward them, her arms outstretched. "Lucy! Stella!"

Wings flapping, the squawking ducks skittered away across the surface of the pond. Ethan got out of the truck and closed the door with a soft click.

Lucy frowned. "Mommy, you scawed dem."

Amber swept her children into an embrace, clutching them to her chest. "How could you scare me like this, girls? I've been frantic. What were you thinking? How—"

"You're squeezing me, Mommy." Stella wriggled in her arms. "I can't breathe."

Amber loosened her hold but only slightly. "Why, girls?" Crouching, she searched their faces. "Why did you run away?"

Stella glanced over Amber's shoulder. "Ethan. Ethan." Wrenching free, she hurled herself at him. Lifting a crying Lucy, Amber turned.

He caught her daughter in his arms. "Why, Stella?

Why would you hurt your mommy like this? We were both so… So…"

Ethan buried his face into Stella's hair, but not before Amber glimpsed the moisture welling in his hazel eyes.

He swiped the tears off his face. "Tell me, sweetheart." With his thumb and forefinger, he lifted her chin to meet his gaze. "Why did you and Lucy run away? We— I was so worried."

Stella's body shuddered with sobs. "I'm sorry, Ethan. I'm sorry, Mommy."

"I'm sowee, too, Mommy…" Lucy wailed, dissolving into a fresh round of tears. "I'm sowee, Efan." Letting go her hold around Amber's neck, Lucy strained toward him.

They loved him so much. Why had she even considered keeping them from him? But she knew. Because she was afraid—terrified—of the way he made her feel. She'd been protecting herself at their expense.

He gathered Lucy close. And the four of them became one unit. Something altogether beautiful.

A family.

Amber's heart sped up at his proximity. How had she thought she—much less the twins—could ever bear to be parted from him?

Then he let go of Lucy—and her—pulling back a pace. Unlatching the tailgate, he set Stella down, and Amber deposited Lucy beside her sister.

Now that her initial fear had abated, Amber planted her hands on her hips. "Where did you think you were going? Anything could've happened to you out here alone. And there wouldn't have been anyone to help you."

"We had to say goodbye to the ducklings," Stella whispered.

"And now Mommy's mad…" Lucy tuned up as if to wail again.

"Mommy has every right to be angry." Ethan's mouth flattened. "I'm feeling none too happy with the two of you myself."

Their faces fell at the gruffness of his tone.

Amber could feel herself starting to shake. The adrenaline that had coursed through her body now exited her limbs, leaving her trembling.

His hand went to the small of her back. "They're safe. Breathe, baby. Breathe. It's okay."

She blinked rapidly.

Lucy tilted her head. "Mommy's not a baby, Efan."

His gaze became steel. "And neither are you two. You're both old enough to remember Mommy told you never to go anywhere without telling her first. This kind of behavior is not acceptable, girls. Running off is definitely not okay."

She sagged against the truck. This was Ethan having her back. Not making her always be the enforcer. Shouldering the parenting alongside her.

Lucy rubbed her eyes. "But we heard you awe-gu-ing."

Stella dropped her chin. "Mommy said she couldn't ever be happy again."

Amber's eyes cut to him. "I never said that. Did I?" Comprehension dawned. "I said…" She gulped.

"You said we could never be happy together." He looked away.

"Because of us," Lucy said.

She squeezed Lucy's hand. "No."

He placed his palm on Stella's head. "Not because of you two."

She and Ethan exchanged a long look.

His Adam's apple bobbed. "Never because of you, Lucy and Stella. None of this is your fault."

Inserting herself on the tailgate between the twins,

Amber placed an arm around each of them. "This is my fault."

"It's nobody's fault," he grunted.

Lucy grabbed hold of his shirttail. "Don't you wuv us anymore, Efan?"

Dwight's SUV lumbered into the clearing.

"I will always love you, Lucy Lou." Ethan touched the tip of her nose. "I will always love you, Stella Bella." His hand cupped her cheek. "But sometimes..." His voice deepened to a gravelly rasp. "Sometimes things don't work out the way we hope."

Dwight got out of the SUV.

Ethan moved aside, putting more than physical distance between them. "Since your dad's here, Amber, it might be better if you rode home with him. He'll be concerned."

At the look on Ethan's face, her heart leaped into her throat. *I've lost him. He's leaving. What have I done?*

Coming alongside, Dwight lifted Lucy and then Stella, placing them on their feet. He hugged them.

Amber jumped off the tailgate to the ground. "Ethan..."

He shook his head, his features suddenly fierce. "We might never be the family I hoped for, but I'm not leaving Truelove."

"What do you mean?"

"I mean Grandma is staying, and so am I. We both love Lucy and Stella. And if you'll allow me, I'd like to be a permanent part of their lives. To be here for them."

She'd been so wrong. Ethan was nothing like Tony.

"But your job... You were looking forward to working in your buddy's boat shop on the coast."

"I'm thinking my granddad's business would suit me

fine." He slammed the tailgate shut. "Kids need a dad, Amber."

The remembered anguish in his voice broke her heart.

He staggered toward the driver's side. "And I may not be your idea of father material, but I aim to be there for them any way I can."

"But you hate Truelove, Ethan."

"I don't hate Truelove. Truelove is home. I've realized home is more than the place where people love you." His gaze locked on to hers. "Home is the place where the people you love live. And I love Lucy, Stella, Grandma and you. Because of that, Truelove will always be my forever home."

Wait. Had he just said…? She blinked at him. He loved her?

Ethan wrenched open the truck door. "I—I've got to go. Take care of my girls, Dwight."

Her father took a step forward. "Ethan…"

"Efan. Efan," Lucy called.

"Don't leave us," Stella cried.

Gazing at them over the bed of the truck, he rested his arms on the frame. "I'll see you little ladies soon. Be good for your mama, okay? But I just…" He gulped. "I just need to check on Grandma."

He threw himself into the truck and sped away.

Something tore in Amber's chest. And it was a moment of clarity. She loved him. With a love far greater than any adolescent crush.

Their own biological father hadn't loved them enough to stick around for their birth, much less anything afterward. Ethan was the kind of man who'd be there for her and the girls. Through thick and thin. The good and the bad. Through the happy times and the sad.

He was a good man. An honorable man. A man she

could trust with the lives of her children. With her heart. He wouldn't leave or desert her when the going got tough.

Dependable. Reliable. Wonderful. She'd never needed to fear him leaving them. She'd never needed to fear letting him into her girls' lives.

Why had she been so foolish to push him away? Her stupid, stupid, abominable pride. She never needed to fear giving him her heart.

God, forgive me. Again.

But would Ethan?

She'd hurt him so badly. Had she lost a chance with him? Had she destroyed everything?

Like his parents, she'd wounded him. Deeply. Beyond repair?

Somehow she had to find a way to convince Ethan that with him her heart found its truest home, too.

Chapter Fifteen

◠

Over the next three days, Ethan did his best to avoid Amber.

Not an easy task in a town the size of Truelove. And not with so many interfering, if well-meaning, match-makers at large. But manage it he did, by sticking to his granddad's workshop and burying himself in a flurry of client orders.

Anything to keep his thoughts from straying to what he'd never have with Amber. Maybe the what-ifs weren't the worst. But the never-could-be's gutted him.

Struggling with a wood joint late Wednesday after-noon, he glanced at the wall where he'd tacked Stella's artwork. The hole in his heart felt huge. Throwing the hammer on the workbench, he swiped his arm across his brow.

On Monday, Amber had started her job at the pedia-trician's office. Her new hours allowed her to not only drop off the girls at school each morning, but pick them up afterward, too.

Who knew he'd miss car pool so much? He shook his head. Which only proved how certifiable he'd become.

Certifiably in love with two little girls and their beautiful mother.

His cell phone buzzed on the table. He frowned. Why
was Miss GeorgeAnne texting him? Urgent. Crisis at the
Mason Jar.

Another text followed on its heels. Mr. Green: A matter of some urgency requires your immediate attention.
Please respond ASAP.

The cell buzzed again. He sighed. Guess who? Emergency. Get your butt to the Jar. Now. Grandma.

His heart quickened. Had something happened to
Grandma? Had she fallen again?

Ethan took off at a run for his truck. All the way into
town, he prayed he wasn't too late. But comforted himself that whatever Grandma's emergency, she'd been well
enough to text. He blew by the sign that said Truelove,
Where True Love Awaits.

He grimaced. He barreled around the town square
and jerked to a stop in one of the empty parking spots
at the Jar.

Throwing himself out of the truck, he raced across
the sidewalk. Why *were* there so many available parking
places in front of the diner? He yanked the door open.
The bell jangled.

He rushed inside only to come to an immediate halt.
He scanned left. He scanned right. The place was deserted. He did a slow three-sixty. What was going on?

Then the door to the kitchen swung open, and Amber
walked into the dining room.

"Where's Grandma? Is she okay?"

Amber wrinkled her brow. "Why do you think—"

"I got a text. Three texts." He clenched and unclenched
his hands. "From GeorgeAnne. IdaLee. And Grandma."

Amber blew a breath between her lips. "Miss Erma-

Jean's fine. I'm so sorry. I never meant to scare you. I should've known better than to get them involved. But they told me they knew how to get you to the Jar. I had no idea they'd—"

"What's this all about, Amber?"

He had an unsettling feeling he'd been the victim of yet another Truelove conspiracy. Although at this point, he wasn't sure what the matchmakers thought to gain. "What did those old women do? Rent out the entire diner?"

Amber gestured to the booth. Their booth. "Since you're here, maybe we could talk?"

He couldn't help but drink in the sight of her. She looked very professional in her lavender-blue scrubs.

"Please, Ethan?"

He dragged his gaze to her face. His heart hammered. He'd never been able to refuse Amber anything, and he didn't aim to start now. So he sat down.

She slipped into the seat across from him. "You're a hard man to track down."

He shrugged. "Been busy. How is your job with the pediatrician?"

"Good."

"And the girls?"

"They're doing well, but missing you." She gnawed her lip. "I miss you."

He missed the three of them so much sometimes it hurt to breathe.

She raised her chin. "I wanted to apologize for the terrible things I said to you."

He let his shoulders rise and drop. "We both said things we shouldn't have."

"I let my fears get the better of me. You are nothing

like Tony or your father." She bit her lip. "Would you forgive me for not trusting you? For not believing you?"

He nodded. "Of course I forgive you." Because when you loved someone, you forgave them.

"Thank you, Ethan." She gave him a tremulous look. "You have no idea how happy I am you decided to stay in Truelove."

His heart already felt lighter. Perhaps to some extent, he would get to remain a part of her life and the twins', after all. Even if it wasn't everything he'd hoped for.

"I'm happy for us to be friends again." He gazed out the window overlooking the square. "The town and the people have a way of growing on a person. I think this is where God wants me to stay, to put down roots."

"You've found a church home here, too. I'm thrilled you've reconnected with old friends and made new friends like Jake and Jonas." She squared her shoulders. "Though of course after everything that's happened, our friendship can't remain as it was."

His throat tightened.

She tilted her head. "What if we decided to not just be friends anymore?"

His heart stuttered. "Then what else would we be, Amber? What do you want us to be?"

Amber bit her lip. "I love you so much it absolutely terrifies me, Ethan."

Something he'd believed frozen in his heart warmed. "You love me?" The buzzing ache in his brain quieted for the first time in three days. The longing in her eyes humbled him.

He swallowed. "Truth is, I think you had my heart from the first moment in the hospital lobby when you said my name."

"I was so focused on my pain that I never stopped to

consider yours. But somewhere inside, I think I've always loved you."

They locked gazes.

She took a breath. "So I'd like to work out a new deal with you, Ethan."

"What are you talking about, Amber?"

"Unlike your previous temporary *arrangement*—" she made air quotes with her fingers "—this deal would be a permanent one."

"Permanent?"

Amber's gaze never left his. "As in forever."

His pulse thundered. In her eyes, there was love. So much love. For him. And a future. The future he wanted more than anything else on earth.

"Exactly what are we talking about here? What are your terms?"

She placed her hands palms down on the tabletop. "What if I promise to never leave you?"

A slow smile spread across his face.

"What if *I* promise to always need you? Because I think we were made for each other. What would you say?"

"I'd say yours might be the one proposal I can't refuse." He cocked his head. "We'd have to think of a way to seal the deal."

"I'm open to negotiation." Her eyebrow hitched. "Do you have something specific in mind?"

Reaching across the table, he took her hand. "I do."

"Something that would signify the binding nature of our agreement." She smiled.

"I like how you think." Letting go of her hand, he leaned against the corner of the booth. "Is there a reason you're still sitting so far away?"

Sliding out of the booth, she eased into the seat beside him. "Not one good reason in the world."

Reaching for her, he just held her in his arms. His breath ragged, he sighed. "That's better." Her shoulder fit in his embrace like she'd been made for him. And he, for her.

"I love you, Amber. So much." He sifted his fingers through the silk of her hair. "I want us to be a family. You, me, Lucy and Stella."

Her eyes were luminous. "Forever."

Ethan trailed his thumb across the apple of her cheek. His mouth found hers. And then he forgot to breathe.

With a final kiss to her closed eyelids, he drew back. "Think your dad will give us his blessing?"

"You've been an honorary family member since Matt dragged you home when you were kids."

"Speaking of kids? What if… What if I didn't just change your last name? How do you think the girls would feel about being Lucy and Stella Green?"

A smile crept across her lovely features. "I think it would be best to let them tell you themselves."

Getting out of the booth, she pulled him to his feet and motioned to someone through the window.

Outside on the sidewalk, Miss IdaLee waved. Miss GeorgeAnne's face wore a *what took you so long* expression. His grandmother had a hand on Lucy's and Stella's shoulders. Blond hair plaited into braids, they were dressed in identical yellow sundresses.

He cut his eyes at Amber. "Pretty sure of yourself."

"Actually, only sure of my heart." She bit her lip. "But I hoped. You gave me back my hope, Ethan."

Kissing her forehead, he vowed to spend his life making sure her dreams came true.

He gave her a crooked smile. "Good to know we've got the matchmakers' seal of approval."

"Are you kidding?" She nudged him with her hip. "I

have it on good authority they've already contacted a wedding photographer."

He laughed. "Do we get to decide anything?"

"The wedding date." She wrapped her arms around his waist. "And how happy we'll be."

"A done deal." He grinned. "Because we're going to be very happy."

The bell over the door jangled.

Shooing the twins over the threshold, his grandmother's gaze cut to him and Amber. "I'm trusting you two can take it from here."

Ethan gave a mock sigh. "Other worlds to conquer, eh?"

Grandma winked at him. "Other matches to make." The bell jangled once more as she rejoined her friends. Laughing and chatting, the three old ladies headed down the block.

Hands behind their backs, the girls hunkered inside the door.

"Lucy? Stella?" He crouched, and they flew into his arms.

Thank You, God. He glanced at Amber. *Thank You for all my girls.*

Wriggling free, Stella thrust a bright blue piece of construction paper in his face. "This is for you."

Amber helped Lucy hop onto a stool.

He examined Stella's picture. In crayon, she'd drawn six stick figures against a backdrop of wavelike mountain ridges. A lump grew in his throat when he saw what she'd painstakingly written at the bottom.

MY FAMILY
BY
STELLA

"Me and Lucy." She pointed out helpfully at the two smallest figures. "Grandpa and Gigi are there."

She looked at him from those solemn little eyes of hers. "Here's Mommy and… Mommy and… Lucy!" Stella hissed. "It's your turn. Pay attention."

Lucy hopped off the stool. "We wuv you, Efan."

He gathered both girls close, but Stella blew out an exasperated sigh. "That's not what you were supposed to say, Lucy. We practiced."

Lucy snuggled against him. "I'm too shy, Stehwaa."

He bit back a laugh.

Smiling, Amber shook her head. "Absolutely untrue."

"Why do I have to do everything in this family?" Stella captured his face and held it between her hands. "Ethan Todd Green?"

"Yes, ma'am?" He didn't have to wonder where she'd learned that—thank you very much, Grandma Hicks.

"Will you marry our mommy, Ethan, and promise to be our forever daddy?"

Tears stung his eyes. His Marine buddies wouldn't have recognized him. The girls—his girls—had turned him into an emotional basket case. And he loved it. Every single minute of it.

"Stella Bella. Lucy Lou." He mouthed, *I love you*, to their mother. Then he hugged the twins tight. "I will."

There was nothing he wanted more than to be a forever daddy. A forever husband. And forever home.

* * * * *

*If you loved this book,
be sure to check out Lisa Carter's
other heartwarming stories:*

His Secret Daughter
Hometown Reunion
The Christmas Baby
The Bachelor's Unexpected Family
The Deputy's Perfect Match

*Find these and other great reads
at www.LoveInspired.com.*

Dear Reader,

Welcome to Truelove, North Carolina—Where True Love Awaits, set in the breathtaking Blue Ridge Mountains of North Carolina.

The course of true love doesn't always run smooth, but never fear. The Truelove Matchmakers will make sure everyone finds their happily-ever-after.

Amber is afraid that she's messed up so badly she will never find love again. Yet when she chooses forgiveness, she finds true freedom.

For Ethan, trust doesn't come easily, either. Because he finds the courage to open his heart to Lucy and Stella, he and Amber find their happily-ever-after as a family.

No matter how tragic the past or present, God can take what is broken and make it into something beautiful. He delights in bringing beauty out of brokenness. For truly, God is the happily-ever-after for which we were made.

I hope you have enjoyed this journey with Amber, Ethan, Lucy and Stella. I would love to hear from you. Email me at lisa@lisacarterauthor.com or visit www.lisacarterauthor.com.

In His Love,
Lisa

COMING NEXT MONTH FROM
Love Inspired®

Available October 15, 2019

THE CHRISTMAS COURTSHIP
by Emma Miller
Caught up in a scandal in her Amish community, Phoebe Miller moves to her cousin's farm in Delaware hoping for forgiveness and a fresh start. The last thing Phoebe expects is to fall for bachelor Joshua Miller. But can their love survive her secret?

HER AMISH CHRISTMAS CHOICE
Colorado Amish Courtships • by Leigh Bale
Inheriting a shop from her grandfather could solve all of Julia Rose's problems—if Martin Hostetler will renovate it. As an *Englischer*, romance with the Amish man is almost impossible, especially with her mother against it. But Martin and his faith are slowly starting to feel like home...

WESTERN CHRISTMAS WISHES
by Brenda Minton and Jill Kemerer
Homecomings bring love for two cowboys in these holiday novellas, where a woman gets more than she bargained for with a foster teen to care for and a handsome cowboy next door, and a bachelor finds an instant family with a single mom and her little girl.

THE TEXAN'S SURPRISE RETURN
Cowboys of Diamondback Ranch • by Jolene Navarro
Returning home with amnesia years after he was declared dead, Xavier De La Rosa is prepared to reconnect with family—but he's stunned to learn he has a wife and triplets. Can he recover his memory in time to reunite his family for Christmas?

HIS CHRISTMAS REDEMPTION
Three Sisters Ranch • by Danica Favorite
Injured at Christmastime, Erin Drummond must rely on her ex-husband's help caring for her nephews. But as they stay on the ranch together, can Erin and Lance find a way to put their tragic past behind them and reclaim their love?

HOMETOWN CHRISTMAS GIFT
Bent Creek Blessings • by Kat Brookes
The last person widow Lainie Dawson thought to ask for help with her troubled child is her brother's friend Jackson Wade—the man she once loved. But when her son bonds with Jackson and begins to heal, Lainie must confront her past—and future—with the man she never forgot.

LOOK FOR THESE AND OTHER LOVE INSPIRED BOOKS WHEREVER BOOKS ARE SOLD, INCLUDING MOST BOOKSTORES, SUPERMARKETS, DISCOUNT STORES AND DRUGSTORES.

LICNM1019

Get 4 FREE REWARDS!

We'll send you 2 FREE Books plus 2 FREE Mystery Gifts.

Love Inspired® books feature contemporary inspirational romances with Christian characters facing the challenges of life and love.

FREE Value Over **$20**

YES! Please send me 2 FREE Love Inspired® Romance novels and my 2 FREE mystery gifts (gifts are worth about $10 retail). After receiving them, if I don't wish to receive any more books, I can return the shipping statement marked "cancel." If I don't cancel, I will receive 6 brand-new novels every month and be billed just $5.24 for the regular-print edition or $5.99 each for the larger-print edition in the U.S., or $5.74 each for the regular-print edition or $6.24 each for the larger-print edition in Canada. That's a savings of at least 13% off the cover price. It's quite a bargain! Shipping and handling is just 50¢ per book in the U.S. and $1.25 per book in Canada.* I understand that accepting the 2 free books and gifts places me under no obligation to buy anything. I can always return a shipment and cancel at any time. The free books and gifts are mine to keep no matter what I decide.

Choose one:
☐ **Love Inspired® Romance Regular-Print**
(105/305 IDN GNWC)

☐ **Love Inspired® Romance Larger-Print**
(122/322 IDN GNWC)

Name (please print)

Address _____ Apt. #

City _____ State/Province _____ Zip/Postal Code

Mail to the Reader Service:
IN U.S.A.: P.O. Box 1341, Buffalo, NY 14240-8531
IN CANADA: P.O. Box 603, Fort Erie, Ontario L2A 5X3

Want to try 2 free books from another series? Call 1-800-873-8635 or visit www.ReaderService.com.

Cash remembered coming out to Ma Dixie's place at Christmas time growing up. The contrast with his own foster family's home had been extreme. There, six themed Christmas trees were spread throughout the house, decorated perfectly by the commercial operation that brought them out each year and took them away after the holidays. That same company had wrapped garlands around the staircase and strung lights outside the house.

It had all been grand. He remembered being shocked and impressed his first year with the family, because it had been so different from the humble holidays back in Alabama. But he hadn't been allowed to invite his brothers over; too much noise and mess, his foster mother had always said. If he wanted to see them, he had to find a ride out to Ma Dixie's, which he had done frequently.

Here, Christmas really felt like Christmas.

He opened another box of ornaments, pulled out an angel made of hard plastic and handed it to Holly to place on the tree.

"Is this your tree topper, Ma?" Holly asked, holding it up.

"Yes, it is. I usually have Pudge put it up, but…could you do it, Cash, honey?"

He did, easily reaching the top of the small tree. "Is Pudge okay?" he asked Ma. "Is that why the place isn't decorated yet? He's too sick to help?"

Ma arranged the last figures in the Nativity scene and sank down onto the couch. "That's part of it. Mostly, it's me feeling blue. I'm not used to Christmas with no kids around."

Holly tilted her head to one side. "Did you have a lot of kids?"

"Dozens," Ma said with a wide smile. "That's the beauty of being a foster parent."

"Oh," Holly said as she sank down onto an ottoman beside Ma. "Do you...not foster anymore?"

Ma sighed. "I really can't with Pudge having all these doctor appointments. I guess maybe we're getting too old for it." She looked wistfully at the tree. "I just, you know, always enjoyed having the little ones around."

Holly looked thoughtful. "Is that why you wanted to take care of Penny? Not to help me out, but to have a little one around?"

"That's part of it," Ma said, "but don't you worry about it. I understand being picky where your child is concerned."

"It's not pickiness," Holly said. "If I were being picky, who better than an experienced foster parent like you?" She reached out and rubbed Ma's arm back and forth, two or three times, an affectionate gesture that made Ma smile.

Cash came over and sat at Holly's side, leaning against the ottoman. His heart, like that of the Grinch in the movie playing muted on the television, seemed to be expanding.

He'd taken plenty of women to high-end Christmas parties and fancy restaurants. But sitting here in Ma Dixie's house, talking with her about holidays and kids and family problems, decorating the tree with her, felt different. Like coming home.

Like coming home, with Holly beside him.

He put that feeling together with the questions his brother and Pudge had been asking. He was getting the horrifying notion that he might be falling in love with Holly. But he wasn't the falling-in-love type, or the settling-down type. And Holly wasn't the type for a short, superficial fling.

So what exactly was he going to do with all these feelings?

Don't miss Lee Tobin McClain's
Low Country Christmas,
available October 2019 from HQN Books!

PHLTMEXP1019

Looking for inspiration in tales
of hope, faith and heartfelt romance?

Check out **Love Inspired**® and
Love Inspired® **Suspense** books!

New books available every month!

CONNECT WITH US AT:

Facebook.com/groups/HarlequinConnection

 Facebook.com/HarlequinBooks

 Twitter.com/HarlequinBooks

 Instagram.com/HarlequinBooks

 Pinterest.com/HarlequinBooks

ReaderService.com

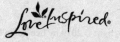

LIGENRE2018R2

Love Inspired®

Discover wholesome and uplifting stories of faith, forgiveness and hope.

Join our social communities to connect with other readers who share your love!

Sign up for the Love Inspired newsletter at **LoveInspired.com** to be the first to find out about upcoming titles, special promotions and exclusive content.

CONNECT WITH US AT:

Facebook.com/groups/HarlequinConnection

Facebook.com/LoveInspiredBooks

Twitter.com/LoveInspiredBks

LISOCIAL2019